GUNS ALONG THE BRAZO

GUNS ALONG THE BRAZO

There seems little to connect a hired gun with rustling from the herds driving north through Texas to the rail-heads, but when the owners of two herds are killed, Dan McCoy, Sheriff of Red Springs, has a tough problem on his hands. He finds himself in the position of having to protect the killer from mob violence whilst rustlers are plaguing the herds. When Dan finds the connection and unmasks a scheme for revenge, all is set for the showdown in Red Springs, Texas.

GUNS ALONG THE BRAZO

by

Jim Bowden

Dales Large Print Books
Long Preston, North Yorkshire,
BD23 4ND, England.

British Library Cataloguing in Publication Data.

Bowden, Jim
  Guns along the brazo.

    A catalogue record of this book is
    available from the British Library

    ISBN 978-1-84262-701-3 pbk

First published in Great Britain in 1967 by Robert Hale Ltd.

Published in Large Print 2010 by arrangement with
Mr W. D. Spence

Dales Large Print is an imprint of Library Magna Books Ltd.

Printed and bound in Great Britain by
T.J. (International) Ltd., Cornwall, PL28 8RW

1

Red Springs lay quiet under the hot, afternoon Texas sun. Dan McCoy, the tall, lean sheriff, and his leather-faced, fifty-three years old deputy, Clint Schofield, lounged in chairs outside their office.

'Some hombre doesn't seem to mind the heat,' observed Clint.

Dan raised his head, pushed his sombrero from his eyes and glanced along the main street. A man on a chestnut horse had just reached the edge of town and was riding at a walking pace which hardly stirred the dust. Dan grunted, tipped the sombrero back over his eyes and resumed his dozing.

A few moments passed. Suddenly Clint gripped Dan's arm tightly. The sheriff was jerked out of his half-sleep.

'Butch Mason!' The words escaped with a hiss from between Clint's tight lips.

Dan was suddenly alert. He settled his sombrero more firmly on his head and pushed himself more upright in his chair. The words were synonymous with killer.

Dan had never seen Butch Mason but he knew of his reputation.

'Are you sure?' he asked his deputy.

'Certain,' replied Clint. 'I saw him in Kansas, an' thet's the same hombre thet's ridin' into this town.'

Dan observed the lone rider shrewdly. He saw a short stocky man whose shoulders seemed unnaturally broad. His dark blue shirt and matching levis were dust-covered, as were his high-heeled, black, calf-length boots. A black Stetson crowned his head, and a black neckerchief was tied tightly round his throat. Although the horse bore signs of long travel, Dan could see that it was a magnificent, powerful animal.

Dan's attention riveted on the man whose reputation as a hired killer was well known throughout Missouri, Kansas and into New Mexico.

'So that's Butch Mason,' he muttered.

'Sure is,' said Clint. 'A mean killer who'll hire his guns to anyone if the money is right. He'll even switch sides if he gets a better offer. One of the fastest men who ever threw a gun, but the law has never been able to pin a killing on him. He makes sure the other man draws first an' depends on his speed to win; it has always been a case of self-defence.'

'Then he's clever,' observed Dan.

'Clever an' ice-cool,' said Clint.

Butch Mason pulled his horse to a halt outside the Silver Dollar saloon, slid lightly from the saddle, stretched himself and stepped on to the sidewalk.

'C'm on,' said Dan, pushing himself from his chair as Butch Mason entered the Silver Dollar. 'I'm goin' to take a closer look at Mason.'

'Wonder what he's down here for,' said Clint. 'He's never operated in Texas as far as I know.'

'That isn't to say he won't,' said Dan, 'but the money must be right to bring him this way.' There was a grim look on the sun-tanned, wind-burned face of the sheriff. 'I can't figure who'd want to hire such a man around here.'

The two men shouldered their way through the batwings and strolled across the room to the bar. Dan's steel-blue eyes had taken the scene in at a glance. There were about thirty people, chiefly cowboys and saloon girls, in the room. Most of them were sitting at the small tables which occupied the centre of the saloon. The gambling tables were closed and would not begin picking up their trade until the saloon began to fill during the evening. Butch Mason was leaning on the long mahogany counter, and Dan knew that the killer had been recognised from the attitude of the people in the saloon. There was a certain amount of whispering and many glances were cast in the direction of the man at the counter. There was a certain tenseness in the air which was relieved slightly by the appearance of the lawmen, but the real easing came when a saloon girl, teased by some cowboy, laughed shrilly. Conversation grew louder and the saloon returned to normal.

Dan and Clint reached the bar where it turned at right angles to the wall. The sheriff positioned himself on the short length of counter so that he could survey the full length of the bar and, in particular, the newcomer to Red Springs.

Butch Mason had placed his Stetson on the counter and revealed thick, black, wavy hair which ran into long sidewinders. Mason's face was square with a prominent jaw-bone. His eyes were dark and cold and Dan could see the meanness in them. Butch drained his glass and called for another beer. He untied his neckerchief and wiped his face. As he retied the neckerchief he glanced at Dan.

'Somethin' matter with me, lawman?' The words seemed to snap from his mouth, and Dan detected a note of contempt in his last word.

'Nothing,' replied Dan calmly. 'I just make it my business to take a look at all strangers in town.'

'Wal, now you've seen, quit starin',' rapped Mason. He picked up his replenished glass and took a long drink.

'Staying long in these parts, Mason?' asked Dan.

'Thet's my business,' replied the hired-gun. A smile split his thin lips. 'So you know me?'

'My deputy recognised you when you rode in,' said Dan.

'Good fer the watch-dog,' mocked Mason.

Dan felt Clint bristling under the comment and knew, in spite of Mason's reputation, Clint would not hesitate to throw a gun on him should circumstances permit.

'Most killers thet I've come across have been full of air; seems to me that you are going to be the same,' said Dan coldly. He smiled to himself when he saw Mason stiffen under the comment. 'Sure I wouldn't have recognised you,' he went on, 'but I've heard of your reputation, an' let me tell you,

Mason, it counts for nothing down here.'

'Big talk, sheriff,' rapped Mason. His eyes narrowed. 'Jes don't let the circumstances arise where you hev to pull a gun on me, for if you do you'll be sayin' goodbye to this world.'

'Mason, I'm concerned with keeping the peace around these parts,' rapped Dan. 'I don't pull a gun unless it's necessary, so it's up to you to see that the circumstances don't arise.' Dan paused to let the full meaning of the words sink in. 'To get back to my question,' continued Dan. 'Are you staying long around here?'

'If it will make you any happier, lawman, the answer is no,' replied Mason. 'I've hed a long ride, stopped here to slake the dust before heading south. That's all, lawman; don't you give anyone a chance around here?'

'Your kind don't seem to want a chance,' countered Dan. 'If you're riding south jest see that it's a long way.' He tapped his deputy on the shoulder. 'C'm on, Clint, let's go.'

Mason said no more, but chuckled to himself as the lawmen strode from the saloon.

Once outside, Dan stopped. 'Go back to the office, Clint, and keep watch for Mason leaving. I'm going to get my horse.'

Before Clint could question him Dan walked away, heading for the livery stable. The grey-haired deputy watched him go. There was a troubled look in his eyes. He loved the young sheriff as if he were his own son. Having served as deputy to Dan's father, Clint was very close to the McCoy family, and, whilst he had great faith in Dan's ability to look after himself, he knew Mason's reputation was not ill-founded and Clint hoped Dan would not have to mix it with the hired killer. Clint knew that many men had been deceived by Dan's leanness and that his quickness on the draw was second to none around Red Springs, but, even so, he was worried as he crossed the road to the sheriff's office.

'I'd like my horse, Zeke,' said Dan when he strode into the livery stable.

'Sure, Dan,' replied Zeke, and hurried to a stall in which a dark, powerful horse was already saddled. When the weather was so hot Dan liked to leave his horse in the capable hands of the stableman, and Zeke always had the animal ready for instant action. 'Thet sure is a nice animal thet's jest been ridden into town,' observed Zeke, when he brought Dan's horse to him, 'but it could do with my attention for a while; it's

13

been ridden far.'

Dan nodded, patted his horse affectionately, thanked Zeke and led the animal from the stable. When he saw that Mason's horse was still outside the Silver Dollar he led his mount to the rail in front of his office. Slipping the reins round the wood Dan walked inside to join Clint.

'He's still in there,' commented the deputy.

Dan nodded but said nothing. Clint eyed him for a moment before speaking.

'What are you figurin' on doin'?' he asked.

The worried state in Clint's voice was not lost on Dan. He smiled as he looked at Clint. 'Nothing desperate,' he replied. 'I'm only going to keep an eye on Mason when he leaves town. I want to see if he was lying when he said he was just passing through here.'

'Be careful, Dan,' said Clint. 'Thet mean streak in Mason could tempt him to provoke you into drawing on him.'

'I'll be all right,' smiled Dan. 'I'm the law around here and I figure it's my duty to keep an eye on characters like Mason. If he behaves himself then there'll be no trouble, but if he steps out of line...' Dan left the sentence unfinished knowing full well that

Clint understood his meaning. 'Besides, why be worried about Mason? I reckon all his kind have reputations bigger than themselves.'

'He's fast, faster than...' muttered Clint, but before he finished his sentence Dan cut in.

'He's leaving!' he said.

Both men watched from the window and saw Butch Mason pause on the sidewalk, then step to his horse and untie it from the rail. He walked it to a water-trough and, after the animal had had its fill, he mounted and rode slowly along the east road out of Red Springs. Dan waited until he estimated Mason had reached the edge of town, then left the office, mounted his horse and turned it in the same direction as that taken by Mason. He was in time to see Mason putting his horse into a gentle trot. Dan hung back but kept Mason in sight as he headed eastwards.

The pace indicated that Mason was in no hurry and, when he swung southwards at the fork in the trail, Dan began to think that Mason had told the truth. However, Dan decided to follow as far as the Brazo River. About three miles further on the trail ran close to some hills then swung sharply round the bluff to start a gradual descent to the Wayman's Ford crossing of the Brazo. When he turned the bluff Dan saw that Mason was no longer in sight. Almost at the same instant as he realised this a voice rasped behind him.

'All right, lawman, freeze!'

Dan stopped his horse instantly and stiffened in the saddle. The threat in Mason's voice told Dan that a Colt was pointing straight at his back and that if he made a move towards his gun he would be blasted out of the saddle.

Mason stabbed his horse forward until he was alongside the sheriff.

'You came to the saloon to look me over, now you tail me; what goes with you?' asked Mason, his lips drawn tightly back.

'I'm not following you,' replied Dan, 'I'm on my way to the Bar X ranch to see my father-in-law. That's it over there.' Dan nodded in the direction of a group of buildings situated close to the Brazo which lay about three miles away.

'A likely story,' mocked Mason.

'It's true,' said Dan, 'and to prove it you can ride along with me.'

'You choose a strange time to pay him a visit,' said Mason suspiciously, 'just after I

16

leave town, an' incidentally your horse wasn't outside your office when I arrived in town yet it was there when I rode out; seems to me that you collected it an' then waited for me to leave.'

Dan's face was impassive although he was surprised at the shrewdness of this man. He had figured things correctly, but Dan was not going to let him know it.

'Coincidence,' said Dan. 'Now if you're finished I'm pushing on to keep that appointment.' Mason looked at Dan curiously and threatened him with his Colt. Dan smiled. 'You won't shoot me,' he went on. 'I'm not going to draw on you, as much as you might like it; you haven't broken the law around here. I suppose you could shoot me in cold blood and claim self-defence; there are no witnesses; but I figure you won't do that. You'd have my deputy dogging your trail for the rest of your life. Your sort like to do the trailing; you don't like anyone to be on your back; it gets you too jumpy, and that's fatal to a gunman.' Dan paused and looked hard at the hired-gun. 'Jest keep riding south and everything will be all right.'

Dan kicked his horse forward and shoved it into a gallop towards the Bar X. He knew his back was broad to the muzzle of the Colt in Mason's hand, but, as he figured, the bullet never came.

When Dan pulled up outside the long, low, wooden ranch-house his father-in-law was there to meet him.

'Hello, Dan,' greeted the black-haired, weather-beaten Bill Collins. 'What brings you out here?'

'I used you as an excuse,' replied Dan. 'I've been trailing Butch Mason.'

'Butch Mason!' exclaimed Collins. 'You mean *the* Butch Mason from Kansas?'

'The same man,' said Dan. 'That's him heading for the ford.' He indicated the lone horseman, a small figure in a vast stretch of country, who was riding towards Wayman's Ford about two miles along the Brazo from the Bar X.

'What's he doing down these parts?' asked Bill, a frown creasing his brow.

Dan told his father-in-law of the encounter with Butch Mason in Red Springs.

'Let's hope he keeps riding,' commented Collins when Dan had finished his story. 'Wherever Mason is there's trouble.'

The two men leaned on the rail of the verandah watching the horseman move steadily towards the river. Five minutes passed then the sound of an approaching horse drew their attention. They glanced round to see Howard, Bill Collins's son, approaching. The tall, broad-shouldered, fair-haired man pulled his horse to a halt, swung quickly from the saddle and stepped on to the verandah.

'Hello, Dan,' he greeted pleasantly. 'You both look preoccupied with that rider. Who is he?'

'Butch Mason,' answered Dan.

It was Howard's turn to be surprised, and Dan quickly recounted his meeting with Mason.

The rider had reached the river by this time and the three men saw him hesitate a few moments before putting his horse into the water.

'Well, I guess maybe he was telling the truth,' observed Dan. 'I thought for a minute he was gong to turn around when he reached the water.'

'The river is running high after the recent rains they've had further west,' said Bill. 'I guess that's why he hesitated. By the way, Howard, you'll soon have to be riding out to meet the herds trailing north. When you do you'll have to warn them about the river. Wayman's Ford is the only safe crossing place at the moment; they'd be well advised

19

to use only that crossing. If any herds are getting close to the one in front they had better hang back rather than try to save time by crossing the Brazo elsewhere.'

'The southern cattlemen sure ought to be grateful for all the advanced information you send them,' said Dan.

Whenever cattle herds were trailing north to the Kansas railheads Bill Collins always sent someone to meet them with information about the condition of the Brazo and the availability of grazing land, for a stop-over while they replenished supplies in Red Springs. 'Wal,' replied Bill, 'like you, I think it's better if we cattlemen hang together.'

The three men went into the house. Dan gave Bill news of the latest improvements on his own ranch, the Circle C, whilst they had a cup of coffee.

'Dan,' said Howard, interrupting the trend of the conversation, 'I've been thinking about Mason and wondering if there's any connection between him and the three rough lookin' characters I saw encamped five miles west of here in Whispering Hollow.'

'When did you see them?' asked Dan.

'This morning,' replied Howard. 'I've just ridden in from that part of the range. Their camp was fresh, but I figure they might be staying the rest of the day.'

'Did you question them?' asked his father.

'Had no cause to,' answered Howard. 'They didn't see me, but they were three of the toughest looking types I've seen round these parts for some time.'

'Well, we get them passing through when the herds are coming north,' pointed out Bill Collins. 'They drift down from the north hopin' to pick up jobs pushin' cattle back to their own state. After days on the trail they probably look rougher than they are.'

'It's probably as you say,' said Dan, 'but I think I'll look them over.'

He bade his father-in-law and brother-in-law goodbye and rode at a steady pace away from the Bar X. After riding for half a mile he decided to go back to Red Springs and take Clint with him to Whispering Hollow. Clint had recognised Butch Mason; maybe he would know the three men in Whispering Hollow.

Clint Schofield was relieved when he saw Dan riding along the main street.

'Glad to see you back,' greeted Clint. 'Did Mason keep riding?'

'Yes,' replied Dan, 'right across the Brazo. Get your horse, Clint, we've got some investigating to do at Whispering Hollow. Howard saw three rough looking characters camped there. I thought we'd look them over.'

Clint nodded and headed for the livery stable, and the two lawmen were soon heading out of Red Springs.

When they neared the hollow Dan slowed the pace to walking speed and at a point where the ground began to slope gently downwards, he pulled to a halt.

'I'll take a look before we ride in,' said Dan. He threw his reins to Clint. 'You stay with the horses.' Dan slipped from the saddle and started down the slope. Fifty yards ahead the slope steepened sharply and, when he neared this sudden alteration in the terrain, Dan dropped to his stomach, removed his Sombrero and crept forward. He moved very cautiously and when he reached the edge of the hollow he found himself looking down to the encampment. A pot was boiling on a small fire and three men lounged on the ground in the shade of a group of boulders. There was nothing unusual to raise Dan's suspicions as he crawled away from the edge of the steep slope and, when he rose to his feet, waved Clint forward. The deputy pulled to a halt beside Dan, who swung into the saddle. They turned their horses to the left and thirty yards further on swung into the hollow.

The noise of the horses as they negotiated the slope startled the three men. They sprang to their feet, and Dan noted their hands automatically closed round the butts of their Colts, but when they saw the stars pinned to the shirts of the horsemen they relaxed. Dan and Clint pulled to a halt in front of the three men. The sheriff summed them up in a glance. Howard was right; they were three rough-necks. They were in need of a shave and their clothes were dirty, but Dan noted one thing in particular, that the butts of their Colts were smooth from frequent use.

'Howdy,' greeted one of the men pleasantly with a smile which revealed a row of uneven, yellowing teeth.

Dan acknowledged the greeting. 'Strangers around these parts, aren't you?' he said.

'Yeh,' came the reply, 'but we haven't done anything agin' the law.'

'We aren't hounding anyone,' replied Dan. 'We were just passing, saw your camp, and were naturally curious to find strangers camping outside of town.'

'There's nothing mysterious about that,' answered the man. 'We've done a lot of travellin' from Kansas an' I figured on easing up during the hottest part of the day.'

'Where are you heading?' queried Dan.

'South, hoping to help push a herd back north,' came the reply.

Dan nodded. 'Well, I guess we'll move on,' he said and, with a glance at Clint, turned his horse towards the slope.

Once they were clear of the slope Clint pulled alongside Dan.

'They were unknown to me,' he said. 'But they sure were a rough crew, an' I reckon they aren't just satisfied with pushing steers.'

Dan agreed. 'I wonder if there is any significance in the fact that they have come from Kansas; Butch Mason operated there.' Dan shrugged his shoulders. 'Maybe we are being too suspicious,' he added.

The two lawmen pushed their horses into a steady lope and headed for Red Springs.

2

Two days later, Dan was working in his office when his attention was drawn by the pound of hoofs in the main street. He pushed himself to his feet and crossed to the window.

'Somebody in a mighty hurry,' said Clint, as he put down the rifle he was cleaning, and joined the sheriff beside the window.

'Sure is,' agreed Dan, when he saw a dust-covered cowboy starting to haul on the reins as he neared the sheriff's office. 'C'm on, this smells of trouble.'

The two men hurried outside to find the dust swirling under the sliding hoofs of a sweat-lathered horse. The young, weather-beaten cowboy almost tumbled out of the saddle when he tried to dismount, and it was obvious that he had had a hard ride.

'Glad to find you here, Sheriff,' panted the rider, whose legs began to give way with cramp.

Dan and Clint moved swiftly to his side and helped him into the office. The cowboy flopped on to a chair and, whilst Dan began to massage the newcomer's legs vigorously, Clint took a bottle of whisky from the cupboard and poured out a drink.

'Trouble,' gasped the cowboy.

'Take it easy for a minute, son,' said Clint, handing him the glass.

'Thanks,' said the man gratefully. He waited for a few moments while he regained some of his breath, then he drank the whisky.

'That's better,' he said. 'Thanks, Sheriff,

my legs will be all right.'

Dan smiled and stood up. 'Feel ready to talk now?'

The young man nodded. 'I'm Chuck Sanders,' he said. 'I ride for Matt Stevens, who's driving a herd north. Last night we bedded the herd down at the south end of Cedar Valley intending to get through the valley today. This morning just before dawn we were raided, the herd scattered and a bunch of them driven off.'

'Rustlers!' gasped Dan. He glanced at Clint in surprise.

'We haven't had rustlers operatin' around here for a long time,' remarked the deputy.

'Did you see any of them?' asked Dan, turning to the cowboy, who had dropped his Stetson on the floor and was wiping his dusty, perspiring face.

Chuck shook his head. 'Not to recognise them,' he answered. 'There wasn't sufficient light and their neckerchiefs were tied across their faces.'

'How many of them?' queried Dan.

'I reckon eight or ten,' replied Chuck.

Dan rubbed his chin thoughtfully; his mind was already racing, wondering if Butch Mason and the three strangers had had anything to do with the rustling.

'I know what you're thinking,' broke in Clint, 'but I think it is very doubtful if Butch Mason had anything to do with the rustling; he's not a cattleman; he lives by his gun.'

Dan nodded and looked at Chuck. 'How many head of cattle did you lose?'

'I don't know,' replied Chuck. 'They were still roundin' up the strays when I left. Mr Stevens told me to get here as quickly as I could to let you know what had happened. He also wants to know if there is any chance of protection as far as Red Springs.'

'I don't think the rustlers will hit the same herd again,' said Dan. 'They will know that you'll be on look out for them. However, I won't ignore Stevens's request altogether.' Dan turned to Clint. 'Howard will be riding south on his usual trip to advise the herds about the Brazo; it might be a good idea if you rode along with him.'

'Right,' agreed Clint. 'I'll see if I can find any clues out there. I reckon the rustlers might wait to try the same thing on the next herd.'

'I'll ride with you to the Bar X. Will you get the horses and see if old Zeke has a fresh one for Chuck? He can change it for a cattlewise pony from the remuda when he gets back to the herd.'

When Clint had left the office Dan took Chuck to another room. 'You can have a clean-up here,' he said, indicating the water and towel, 'then I'll take you for a meal before we ride out to the Bar X.'

'Thanks,' said Chuck, and within the hour he felt recovered from his hard ride.

When the three men arrived at the Bar X they found that Howard Collins had arranged to leave on his trip the following day, but when Dan explained the situation he agreed to leave immediately. He made preparations quickly, and an hour later Clint, Howard and Chuck bade Dan goodbye and headed across the Brazo. Dan knew that they would not get there before dark but, unless Chuck felt the strain too much, they would ride far into the night.

The three men kept to a steady pace and it was close on midnight when Clint decided that it would be too much for Chuck, willing as he was, to ride all the way to the herd. They were soon rolled in their blankets and, though Clint had them back in the saddles by five in the morning, they felt much better for their rest. They immediately settled into a fast pace so that they would cover most of the distance before the heat of the day. The hills were soon in sight and they were well on their way through Cedar Valley when they saw the cowboys riding point and behind them the bellowing herd of steers sending a cloud of dust billowing skywards.

One of the point riders suddenly put his horse into a gallop in their direction. It was obvious that he had recognised Chuck again, when, some distance away he pulled his horse to a halt, let out a loud whoop and waved his Stetson. He wheeled his horse quickly and put it into a fast gallop towards the herd. It was not long before the three men saw him returning with another rider.

'He's bringin' Matt Stevens,' commented Chuck.

'Howdy Clint, Howard,' greeted Matt Stevens, recognising the two men from his previous trail drives north, when the five riders pulled to a halt. 'You made good time, Chuck. Any more men comin'?' he added, glancing at Clint.

'Dan figures you'd be too alert for the rustlers to hit you again,' said Clint.

'Maybe he's right,' agreed Stevens. 'I doubled the guard last night and we haven't seen any more of the rustlers.'

'Howard was doing his usual trip to the trail herders,' said Clint, 'and Dan reckoned I might as well ride along. We'll ride back with you through the valley and if you agree Howard and I will patrol on either side of the valley.'

'Sure; work it how you like,' said the broad-shouldered, thick-set Stevens. He was a powerfully built man with muscular arms and broad hands, but they were hands with a light touch which his cow-ponies readily answered. His face, chiselled by the weather of ten long drives into Kansas, broke into a smile. 'My main interest is to get this herd through, and I'll leave the rustlers to you lawmen.'

'Right,' said Clint. 'I'll take the west side, you take the east side, Howard. I suggest we move a little ways up the hillside; we'll have a better supervision of them there. Two shots if you see anything suspicious.'

With plans made, the group split up, and Howard and Clint moved off on their patrols. Throughout the day Clint kept an unceasing watch and he kept catching sight of Howard roaming backwards and forwards on the opposite hillside. Below him, Matt Stevens pushed the herd as fast as he could. He wanted to get through the fourteen-mile valley before nightfall and that meant an all-out effort by all the drovers.

Clint was always thrilled by the sight of a

herd with three or four thousand steers on the move, and he never ceased to admire the toughness of the drovers, who, in all weathers and against all conceivable kinds of obstacles, kept the cattle moving. Fights with Indians, stampedes, raids by rustlers, swollen rivers or parched tracts of country all came alike to this breed of men who, throughout every adversity, kept a watchful eye on the herd he was paid to get safely to the railhead or grazing grounds in the north. About mid-day Clint dropped into the valley to ride to the chuck-wagon which had gone on ahead. The cook would have a meal ready so that the drovers could ride in in turn whilst the others kept the herd moving. It was only a matter of a quick snack, then back in the saddle, and Clint was soon patrolling the hillside again.

The afternoon proved uneventful. By early evening the herd was clear of Cedar Valley. Matt Stevens ordered the herd to be bedded down for the night, about a mile further on, and it was a relieved crew who enjoyed the evening meal round the camp fire after they had swilled off the dust of the day. Stevens invited Clint and Howard to spend the night in camp, and after a day in the saddle both men were pleased with the relaxation of the drovers' camp. As the chill night air made itself felt, the men drew closer to the fire, finding relief to the lonely drovers' life in each other's company as they talked about the girls they had left behind, and yarned about previous drives. The flame shed a dancing light across the lined faces, and across the range the night riders, thinking of the homes behind them, crooned a lonely song to sooth the cattle.

Howard discussed the state of the Brazo with Matt Stevens before turning in and the trail boss was grateful for the information.

'I think Shaun O'Grady's should be the next herd behind me. Apologise for my delay; it will have put him a day closer to me, but if all goes well at the Brazo and I get across quickly there'll be no crowding up,' said Stevens as the two men made for their bed rolls.

'Sure,' replied Howard, and, after bidding Stevens goodnight, he was soon under his blankets.

The camp was awake early the next morning and all was hustle and bustle with the object of getting the herd on the move as soon as possible. After a breakfast of salt bacon and beans, swilled down with hot coffee, Clint and Howard said goodbye to

32

the drovers and headed southwards through Cedar Valley to meet the next herd.

There was a new enthusiasm about the drovers when the herd got under way. They felt that now they were clear of the hills the rustlers would not attack them again, but more than that there was now the prospect of two days' break. If they could cross the Brazo that day the boss was sure to ease up. He would graze the cattle north of the river so that all the drovers could have at least one night in Red Springs. The thoughts of a town, of feminine company and whisky brought a zest from the cowboys which even the Longhorns seemed to feel.

About mid-day Matt Stevens and his scout left the herd in the capable hands of his ram-rod and rode ahead to inspect the Brazo. They returned during the afternoon to report that, although the river was running higher than usual, a crossing was possible and that they would put the cattle straight at the water. The cowboys knew what was expected of them without a lot of detailed instructions. They tightened the herd up, the drag men pushing the strays harder to keep the cattle more compact. Chuck Sanders rode ahead leading the lead steer a short distance in front of the main herd. If the lead steer could be put into the water the rest would follow comparatively easily and one of the main problems, that of getting the steers to face the fast flowing water, would be solved. All would not be over, the cattle would have to be goaded and coaxed, urged to swim against the river. Men would be back and forth across the Brazo forcing the Longhorns across and that was the one thing most drovers hated, the swimming of the river, especially the Brazo with its known toll of victims. The point man kept the front corners of the herd pressed inwards so that the cattle would not spread along the great length of the river. Matt Stevens kept a general eye on things; he was everywhere on his strong Texas pony, but, when the river came in sight, he moved up front within helping distance of Chuck Sanders.

Chuck urged the steer onwards, moving in close, slipping his coiled lariat against his saddle and whooping at the top of his voice. All was going well, the river was getting close when suddenly the lead steer must have realised the fastness of the water. It veered sharply and, as swift as Chuck's pony was to react to the steer's action, it was not quick enough. There was a sickening crash as flesh met flesh and the pony stumbled. Caught unawares by the sudden change, Chuck was thrown from the saddle. He landed heavily on his shoulder, the breath driven from his body. He pushed himself quickly to his feet, but his pony had regained its balance even more quickly and, frightened by what had happened, galloped away in the wake of the steer which had turned parallel to the river. Chuck Sanders found himself on foot in front of the oncoming herd!

Matt Stevens saw what had happened, wheeled his pony swiftly, stabbed it with his heels and put it into a dead run towards Chuck. As soon as they saw Chuck's predicament the men riding point released their pressure on the herd, hoping that with the easing the cattle would begin to spread out and slacken their pace. But the drag men, unaware of what had happened, urged the herd on from behind. It seemed like an age to Matt before he got close to Chuck, who had started to run towards the river. The steers, bellowing and churning up the dust, were closing the gap rapidly as Stevens turned his horse alongside Chuck and pulled up sharply, pausing just sufficiently for Chuck to grasp his outstretched arm and swing up behind his boss. Immediately, Stevens kicked the pony forward and with the earth flying beneath its hoofs headed for the river. The herd thundered behind them, but the cattle in the lead were already beginning to turn to follow the lead steer. The herd swung in a great arc and, when Matt Stevens pulled his mount sharply round close to the water's edge, the steers thundered past only a few yards away.

'Thanks, Boss,' called Chuck breathlessly. 'Sorry to cause such a chaos.' He jumped down from the pony and, with a nod to him, Matt Stevens sent his pony galloping away, bent on the urgent task of turning the herd back towards Wayman's Ford. As soon as the drovers realised that something was wrong, pressure was taken off the back of the herd and cowboys urged their ponies forward to prevent what threatened to become a stampede. By the time Matt Stevens reached the front of the herd his two point men had raced to the lead steer and were beginning to ease its pace and turn it on a course away from the river. Dust arose in a great billowing cloud as the herd began to swing round on itself, and those cowboys who had not already pulled their neckerchiefs over the lower halves of their faces did so to try to keep out some of the choking dust. Matt rode fast, sending his pony first to one point and then to another;

he was on the flank, then up front, yelling his instructions and admiring his quick-thinking outfit which prevented the herd from running too far and had succeeded in preventing the upset from becoming a stampede. Suddenly he was startled when a cowboy, a few yards away, pulled out a gun and loosed off two shots in the air. Matt turned his horse nearer to the man.

'What are you doing?' he yelled, his face black with anger. 'You'll get them stampeding. Put that gun away.'

The only answer from the cowboy was another shot in the air.

'You fool!' shouted Matt, his eyes blazing furiously. 'Holster that gun before I use mine on you!'

Matt was close to the man. He was surprised that he did not recognise him, but in this dust and with a neckerchief over his face, it was hard to recognise anyone. The man fired again. Fury blazed in Matt Stevens; his hand tore at his gun, but as it left its leather, the unknown cowboy fired and at such short range the bullet took Stevens in the heart.

The man glanced round quickly. There was not another rider in sight on this side of the herd. He turned his horse, rode swiftly alongside the steers, and when two riders came across Stevens's body, he had been lost in the dust-cloud before slipping away to the trees beside the river from which he had emerged to join the milling cowboys when they were trying to control the herd.

3

The sun was sinking towards the western horizon when Dan McCoy rode into the drovers' camp to find a depressed group of men. It had been a shock to Dan when one of the drovers had arrived at Red Springs and told him of Matt Stevens's murder. Dan had known Matt for a number of years and admired the trail boss who, whilst being tough and firm with his men, also had their respect.

The ramrod, Batt Chambers, strode to greet Dan as the sheriff swung down from his horse.

'Bad business, Sheriff,' said Batt. 'Sorry there was some delay in letting you know, but we were having trouble with the herd and the Brazo wasn't an easy river to cross today.'

'That's all right,' replied Dan. He purposely declined Batt's offer of a cup of coffee and remained where he was because he wanted to have a word with the ramrod alone. 'Tell me what happened before I speak to the men.'

Batt explained Chuck's accident which caused the herd to veer away from the river. 'We were turning them in upon themselves and were getting them under control when some fool started firing his gun. We could see nothing but the dust cloud, but I started off with Wes in the direction of the firing. We had only gone a few yards when there was another shot, then we came across Matt's body.'

'Did you see anyone?' asked Dan.

'No one,' replied Batt. 'It would be easy for someone to get lost in the dust and milling cattle.'

Dan nodded thoughtfully.

'There was one thing,' went on Batt. 'One of the riders, Jed, saw a horseman against the trees close to the river.'

Dan looked sharply at Batt. 'Did he know him?' he asked eagerly. The ramrod shook his head. 'No, he was too far off and our man was too busy with the cattle at that time. He figured the stranger was probably some local who happened to be this way.'

'Did your man see him before or after the shooting?' queried the sheriff.

'After the shooting,' replied Batt. He saw the surprised look on Dan's face and knew immediately that Dan was wondering why the drover had not given chase. Before Dan could raise a query Batt hastened an explanation. 'Jed heard the shots, but did not know for some time afterwards that Matt had been killed.'

'I see,' said Dan. 'I'll have a word with Jed in a few minutes. I suppose you can account for all your men?'

'Sure,' replied Batt. 'They are all here or bedding down the herd. If you are thinking one of them could hev done it let me assure you that you are wrong. There is not one of them missing and I figure a man who would kill Matt Stevens would make himself scarce. Apart from that, every one of these men has ridden with Matt before, and you know as well as I do that Matt was respected and liked by all the drovers that ever rode these cattle trails.'

'Do you have a theory why your trail boss should be killed?' asked Dan.

Batt was surprised by the question. He looked hard at Dan. 'You're a sheriff,' he countered. 'You're the man that's supposed to find the answer to those sort of questions, but if you mean that I've ridden with Matt for a few years and I might know someone with a grudge, I am afraid I can't help you. What Matt got up to between drives was his business, but I reckon that whoever shot him must have had a grudge.'

'And none of your drovers had, so that leaves the stranger,' said Dan. 'Let's have Jed over.'

Batt nodded and shouted for Jed. A moment later a cowboy ambled up to them.

'Batt tells me you saw a stranger shortly after the shooting,' said Dan.

'Yes,' drawled Jed.

'Do you think he could have got there from the herd without being seen?' asked Dan.

'Sure,' replied Jed without hesitation. 'The cattle were sure creating a dust an' they weren't so far from the trees at that spot. Yes, it would have been possible.'

'You're sure you didn't know him?' queried Dan.

'Yes,' replied Jed. 'An' I only saw his back. Only thing that struck me was that his horse looked a strong, powerful animal.'

'Thanks, Jed,' replied Dan. He looked

thoughtful as Jed walked away.

'I'm sorry we can't be more helpful,' said Batt, 'but there was so much going on that...'

'You've been most helpful,' cut in Dan. 'You've assured me that your drovers are in the clear as far as you are concerned. I'm sure if it was one of them it will come out during the remainder of the drive; that leaves me in the clear to pursue the theory about the stranger; a mighty good job Jed saw him. Are you going to take the herd right through?'

'I will have to,' replied Batt. 'Matt was also keen to serve the ranchers who committed their cattle to him. I won't let him down on this trip. We buried him close to the Brazo beside the trail he used so many times; we thought he'd like that better than in some cemetery. We figured on stopping over a couple of days to give the boys a break in Red Springs, but I reckon none of them will be particular now; we'll push on in the morning.'

'Probably the best thing,' agreed Dan. 'It will keep your men's minds occupied. I hope I will have some news of an arrest when you return this way.'

'You have some idea who it was?' asked Batt keenly.

Dan smiled. 'Well, it's only a theory, but I'm not prepared to discuss it.'

He bade Batt and the drovers goodbye and headed for Red Springs, his thoughts full of a possibility of Butch Mason having doubled back on his tracks. It was a possibility but Dan could find no motive.

When Clint and Howard left Stevens they kept to a steady pace through Cedar Valley. They saw no one all day and had cleared the valley and were five miles across the grassland to the south before they sighted the dust cloud of the next herd. By the time they reached it, the drovers were starting to bed down the herd for the night.

Shaun O'Grady greeted them warmly when they rode into the camp. They were pleased to be out of the saddle and appreciative of the meal which was offered to them. The drovers were eager for news from Red Springs and anxious to know the conditions which lay ahead, especially the state of the Brazo.

'The Brazo's running high,' said Howard, 'but you'll hev to watch out for rustlers before thet. Matt Stevens was hit this end of Cedar Valley.'

'What!' O'Grady was surprised at this news. 'There hasn't been any rustling on this trail for years.'

'Wal, you'll have to be on the look out on this trip,' pointed out Clint. 'I propose to ride back with you while Howard rides south to contact the other herds.'

'Right,' said O'Grady. 'An extra man will be useful.'

'I'll roam ahead if thet's agreeable with you,' said Clint. 'Maybe I can pick up something on these here rustlers.'

'That will be all right by me,' agreed the trail boss.

During breakfast the following morning Clint took O'Grady to one side. 'I don't want to interfere, Shaun,' he said, 'but I've been figurin' thet with the herd placed as it is we will be half-way along Cedar Valley by nightfall tonight, and that won't be a good place to bed down.'

'I've stopped there before,' pointed out O'Grady.

'Yeh, but not with rustlers about,' replied Clint. 'You'll give them a good opportunity to scatter the herd into the hills and then pick up the strays at their leisure.'

'I can't push the herd right through Cedar Valley from here before it's dark,' said O'Grady testily. 'And I'm not hanging back this side of the valley; I don't want to lose any time.'

'But if you…' started Clint.

'We appreciate your concern,' interrupted the trail-boss, a note of annoyance in his voice, 'but I'm in charge of the outfit an' I'm running things my way. We'll deal with the rustlers if they try to hit us.' He turned on his heel and strode away.

Clint shrugged his shoulders and watched him go.

'Trouble?'

Clint glanced round to see Howard beside him.

'Looks as if we're going to be half-way along Cedar Valley tonight,' he explained.

'Well, I sure wouldn't choose that place with rustlers about,' remarked Howard. 'O'Grady always was a determined sort of man who was slow to take advice; always did think he knew best. Wal, best of luck, Clint. I reckon I'll be pushing off.'

The drovers were already getting the herd on the move when Howard bade Clint goodbye and headed south across the grassland. Clint watched his young friend go with mixed feelings and was beginning to wish that Howard was riding with him.

Clint soon had his horse saddled and was riding ahead of the herd of bellowing steers.

When they neared Cedar Valley, Clint rode further ahead and scouted the hills forming the entrance to the valley, but he saw no sign of anyone. However, Clint was not happy. He knew it would be easy for someone to keep the herd under observation whilst keeping out of sight.

'Anything to report?' asked O'Grady when Clint rode into camp as dusk was closing in on the Texas countryside.

'Nothin',' replied Clint, 'but I'll be mighty glad when it's daylight.'

'There's nothing to worry about,' laughed Shaun. 'I've doubled the night riders.' Clouds were gathering in the night sky as the drovers laid out their bed rolls, and, as they thickened, the atmosphere became heavier. It was almost as if there was an uneasiness in the air, a foreboding which the drovers were quick to feel. The cattle did not settle easily, and when, about three o'clock in the morning, thunder rumbled far in the north, they grew restless again. The night riders were thankful that the guard had been doubled and they watched the herd more keenly as the thunder continued to beat the northern skies throughout the early hours. They were thankful the storm came no closer. With the steers so on edge, a

46

louder clap of thunder, a flash of lightning or any unusual sound could start a stampede. The men kept up their ceaseless patrol, round and round the herd, trying to keep the cattle soothed. So intent were they on their task that they failed to notice seven horsemen slip quietly round a spur of a hill on the north side of the herd.

It was just before the first light and the seven men kept close to the dark hillside, impatiently awaiting the prearranged signal. An eighth member of the gang was already in the advanced stages of the plan set for him on the south side of the herd. He had moved quickly to the horses tied to a rope between two stakes and swiftly released the animals. The man had completed his task so deftly that there had been hardly a whinny from the horses and they still remained where they were. The man moved quickly but silently away and once he gained some height on the hillside drew his Colt and loosed off two rapid shots over the horses' heads. Scared by the sudden shattering of the silence under the whine of the bullets close to them, the animals panicked, and finding themselves unsecured, they bolted.

At the sound of the gunfire the seven men knew their companion had been successful and they went into action immediately. They kicked their horses forward and galloped hard at the herd, yelling at the tops of their voices and firing their Colts. Already uneasy at the noise of the thunder, the cattle were quickly thrown into a panic by the rushing, noisy men. The steers nearest to them turned away from the noise. Steer pushed against steer in the attempt to get out of the way. The movement swept through the whole herd swiftly, and the cattle turned and ran. Flesh crashed against flesh, sharp horns ripped through hides, turning fright into terror as the men pressed closer upon them, forcing them onwards.

The attack had been so sudden that the rustlers were on top of the two cowboys, on the side of the herd nearest to them, before they realised it. Flying lead cut them from their saddles before they had time to draw a Colt in self-defence. The two drovers on the far side of the herd tried in vain to stem the rush and were swept out of the way by the stampeding cattle. The sleeping drovers were awakened by the sound of the first two shots, and were startled by the noise of the galloping horses and the gunfire from the direction of the herd.

'Stampede!' The shout ran through the

thin dawn.

Shaun O'Grady led the rush for the horses but pulled up sharply when he realised they were loose and were already galloping away. The drovers turned helplessly. The cattle were already in full run and were heading down the valley towards them.

'The hillside!' yelled O'Grady, and almost as one man the drovers ran for the slope as the herd thundered towards them. One man fell; another stopped to drag him to his feet and they flung themselves onwards. Scrambling up the slope, they turned, gasping for breath, and watched the herd thunder past only a few feet below them. O'Grady watched helplessly, and beside him Clint cursed, to himself, the man who had not taken his advice. He felt that the rustlers had been given the cattle and if O'Grady had not been so stubborn there would have been every chance that the raid could have been foiled. Dust rose as the steers pounded along the valley, and in the faint light it added a screen for the protection of the rustlers. Dim outlines of riders appeared and vanished, but the drovers dare not risk a shot; the horsemen might be their own night riders.

The four drovers who remained in their saddles after the first rush of the stampede tried in vain to check it and, soon realising their task was hopeless, circled quickly to the back of the herd hoping to get at least one rustler and establish an identity. The masked riders had anticipated such a possibility and, when the drovers loomed through the dust, they were met by a withering fire. Two of them met death, whilst the remaining two, wounded in arms and shoulders, realised pursuit would be hopeless and hauled their horses to a halt. As the dust began to settle they saw the rest of the drovers scrambling back down the hillside to the remains of the camp, wrecked by the tearing hooves of the stampeding herd. They turned their horses towards the camp.

'We still hev two boys in the saddle,' said O'Grady when he saw them. He glanced along the valley, feeling utterly dejected at the loss of the cattle. 'Guess we've seen the last of that herd,' he added.

'Let me hev one of those horses,' said Clint. 'Maybe I can trail that outfit.' Suddenly he stopped and halted O'Grady by grasping his arm. 'Maybe you haven't lost them all,' he added, a new excitement in his voice. He pointed in the direction of the herd where he could just make out the figures of the rustlers. They were wheeling away from the cattle, making for the hillside. 'Looks as if they are goin' to let the cattle run themselves out and then pick up what they want.'

'Sure, you could be right,' said O'Grady excitedly. 'The sooner we can round up our horses the better. Sorry, Clint, you'll hev to forgit pickin' up the trail of the rustlers for the moment. I'm going to need these ponies to find the rest of the remuda, fast.'

Protestations sprang to the deputy sheriff's lips, but he stifled them realising that it would be useless to argue with O'Grady; after all he was in his right and his cattle were more important to him than the capture of the rustlers.

O'Grady hurried to meet the two mounted drovers and, when he saw they were wounded, he shouted for his men. Sensing the note of alarm and urgency in O'Grady's voice they ran towards the riders, whom they helped out of the saddles. The trail boss issued orders quickly and, whilst his ramrod returned with the wounded men to what was left of the camp, O'Grady and one of his top riders mounted the two ponies and headed swiftly along the valley.

It was about an hour later when the trail boss let out a whoop of pleasure. 'Sure, there are the beauties,' he yelled, pointing to a group of horses grazing at the end of a cutting into the hills.

'Reckon they had sense to get out of the way of the trampling hooves,' remarked the drover. 'It's sure goin' to save a lot of searchin'.'

The two men spurred their mounts and were soon driving the remuda back towards camp.

The drovers were pleased to see them back so soon and Clint was relieved to see his own horse amongst them. Horses were selected and quickly saddled and before long the whole outfit with the exception of the cook and the cowboy in charge of the remuda were heading south in search of the cattle.

It was about noon when they first sighted the remnants of the herd and O'Grady called a halt. The riders grouped round him as he gave them their instructions.

'The herd looks as if it is well scattered,' he said, 'an' I reckon some of the critters will hev run into the hills. Look out for the rustlers; they may hev already taken their pickings, but keep your eyes open, shoot fast and ask questions afterwards.' He detailed the drovers to various areas and Clint elected to stay with O'Grady in the valley. He figured that if there were any reports of rustlers he would get word quickly by being with the trail boss.

Cowboys ranged along the valley and short distances into the hills, and throughout the afternoon the work of herding the tired steers together went on. It was little after mid-afternoon when O'Grady and Clint were attracted by the pound of a hard-ridden horse and they turned in the saddle to find one of the drovers riding flat out in their direction.

'Trouble,' muttered O'Grady, and the two men sent their horses in the direction of the approaching rider.

When he reached his boss the man hauled on the reins bringing the animal to a sliding, earth-tearing halt.

'Tim and I got jumped by four masked men,' he shouted.

'Where?' asked Shaun, his eyes smouldering angrily.

'We rode up a gulley and found it opened into a quiet little valley. There were about fifty of our steers grazing peacefully and we set about gathering them up. These four hombres surprised us. Tim was killed, but by hard ridin' and good luck I managed to escape an' high tail it back here.'

'This trip has sure cost some lives,'

muttered O'Grady. 'If only I could get my hands on whoever is behind all this.' The tone of his voice left no doubt as to what was in his mind. 'All right, Brett, you'd better stay with the main herd; we'll soon be startin' to drift them towards camp. It won't be any good returning to that valley; the rustlers will be far enough away by now.' The cowboy nodded, but before he could ride away Clint halted him.

'Tell me how to get to that valley, Brett,' said Clint. He looked at O'Grady. 'I guess there might be just a chance that I might pick up the trail of the rustlers from there.'

'Could be,' agreed the trail boss.

Brett gave Clint the necessary directions quickly, and, when he had ridden off to the main herd, Clint turned to O'Grady.

'Don't worry if I don't rejoin you,' he said. 'If I pick up a clue I'll follow it through and it may mean returning to Red Springs for the sheriff and a posse. You'll hev your hands full gitting thet herd through now you're short-handed. I don't think the rustlers will hit you again; I figure they'll hev got what they wanted. Nevertheless, keep a sharp look out.'

'I sure will, Clint,' said O'Grady. 'I regret I didn't take your advice not to bed down the herd in the valley. We would have stood a better chance in more open country, but I figured doubling the guard would be sufficient.'

'Don't reproach yourself,' comforted Clint. 'In open country the herd would have scattered further. Hope to see you in Red Springs,' he added as he flicked the reins and sent his horse in the direction of the hillside from which Brett had ridden.

Clint soon found the valley, and although he used the rest of the daylight attempting to pick up the rustlers' trail, he was unsuccessful. He followed several clues, but each time the trail petered out, and he realised that the men he was trying to find had been shrewd enough to cover their tracks, and lay down false trails. When darkness gathered over the hills Clint made camp, a little disappointed at his lack of success. In spite of feeling weary after a long day in the saddle, sleep did not come easy to Clint. His thoughts were beset by the trouble which had flared up along the Brazo. He felt that this was not just a spasmodic outburst of rustling, but a deliberately planned campaign. Clint turned over in his mind what his action should be the next day, and finally decided that his duty was to the two herds still trailing north towards Cedar Valley. He felt sure the rustlers would attack them, and with this in mind he decided to put the problem to Sheriff Dan McCoy as soon as possible, and suggest that a posse should be arranged to patrol the valley whilst the two remaining herds got through.

The following morning Clint was in the saddle early, cutting through the hills in the direction of Wayman's Ford. It was mid-morning when he topped a rise and pulled his horse sharply to a halt and turned it quickly back below the skyline. A lone cowboy was riding steadily through the valley, and when Clint slipped from his saddle and crept to the top of the rise, excitement seized him. He recognised the rider as Butch Mason! Clint's mind raced. The hired-gun was on the trail which he had planned to ride, a trail which led through the foothills to Wayman's Ford and then to Red Springs. Mason had lied; he was not just passing through the region on his way south. Why was he returning in the direction of Red Springs? Could a hired-gun be connected with the rustlers? Questions poured from Clint's mind as he watched Mason.

Clint waited until the gunman had ridden some distance along the valley before he moved swiftly to his horse, swung into the saddle, slipped quickly over the skyline and began to wind his way down the slope. The deputy sheriff shadowed Mason cautiously, following from one valley to another. Mason rode steadily, and at noon they were heading along a mile-wide valley which opened towards the flat grasslands stretching north to the Brazo. About half a mile from the end of the valley, the trail ran past a long, low, newly-built ranch-house, and Clint was surprised when he saw Mason leave the trail to approach the house. Clint pulled his horse to a halt close to the hillside, wondering if Butch Mason was calling on Sam Brady, a comparative newcomer to the area, for any specific reason.

When Mason halted close to the verandah Sam Brady appeared. The two men held a brief conversation, then Mason rode on to rejoin the trail behind the house. Clint pushed his horse forward, keeping as far from the house as possible. If there was anything between Brady and Mason he did not want to be seen. Clint was puzzled; Mason had ridden as if he knew where he was going, yet to all outward appearances, the stop at the house had been so brief that it appeared as if he was enquiring the way.

Mason swung in the direction of Wayman's Ford and, after crossing it, headed for Red Springs. Clint followed at a safe distance and when he reached the edge of Main Street, Mason was disappearing through the batwings of the Silver Dollar.

4

Dan McCoy gave Clint a warm welcome when he entered the sheriff's office.

'We've had trouble since you left with Howard,' said Dan, as he poured out a cup of coffee for his deputy. 'Matt Stevens was killed down by the Brazo.'

'What!' Clint gasped. 'Did you git the killer?'

'No,' replied the sheriff. 'There was trouble with the herd when they reached Wayman's Ford and in the panic someone shot Matt.'

Dan went on to explain what had happened. 'One of the drovers saw a man down by the river,' concluded Dan, 'but he was too far away to get a description, besides the drover didn't take a lot of notice; he didn't know Matt had been killed at that time. I wonder if Butch Mason is still hanging around.'

'He sure is,' said Clint. Dan stared at the older man, astonishment showing on his face. 'I've trailed him to town; he's in the Silver Dollar now.' Clint told his story of the attack on Shaun O'Grady's herd and how on his way back to Red Springs he had come across Mason.

'I wonder why Mason has returned,' mused Dan on the conclusion of Clint's story, 'but even more intriguing is why did he call on Sam Brady?'

'It was only a brief visit,' pointed out Clint. 'There may be nothing in it, maybe just an enquiry about direction, and yet who knows? I wish I could have got nearer to hear their conversation.'

'You're certain Mason didn't go inside?' asked Dan.

'He never got off his horse,' replied Clint. 'I would have thought if there had been anything between them he would have gone inside.'

'Well, one thing is certain,' said Dan. 'We'll keep a close watch on Mason now he's back in town. I can't see any connection between him and the rustlers, but you never know. We'll keep Brady in mind, too. We don't know much about him; came here a year ago from Kansas and seemed pretty respectable.'

'Kansas!' gasped Clint. 'Maybe that's it; Mason operated there.'

'You could link a lot of men on that flimsy evidence,' pointed out Dan. 'But it's worth keeping in mind. How far away is O'Grady's herd?'

'I could see its dust cloud when I crossed the Brazo,' replied Clint. 'I figure he'll reach the river before nightfall.'

'I think I'll ride out to meet him,' said Dan. 'Keep a watch on Mason, Clint. If he leaves town tail him close, especially if he heads for the Brazo; I don't want a repetition of the Matt Stevens killing.'

After Clint had cleaned up and had a meal Dan, with the knowledge that Mason was still in the Silver Dollar, left Red Springs in the direction of Wayman's Ford. When he approached the ford Dan saw that Shaun O'Grady had ridden ahead of his herd, which was still some distance away on the southern side of the Brazo, and was conferring with Bill Collins on the north bank.

'Sorry to hear you've had a rough trip, Shaun,' said Dan as he pulled to a halt beside the two men. 'Clint rode in this

60

afternoon; told me all about it.'

'We sure hev,' replied the trail boss. 'Did Clint git a line on the rustlers?'

'No,' answered Dan. 'They covered their tracks too well.' He decided to say nothing about Mason. There was no need to cause alarm and suspicion when it might not be warranted.

'I sure hope the next two herds are luckier than I was,' said O'Grady.

'When do you figure Howard should be back?' asked Bill Collins.

O'Grady looked thoughtful. 'If he doesn't stay too long with the herds and does some hard ridin', I reckon he should be back some time tomorrow.'

Bill nodded and turned to Dan. 'We were discussing the crossing when you arrived,' he said.

'Being short-handed has held me up,' said O'Grady. 'I reckon I won't get them all across before nightfall. The boys have had a rough time and I don't want to push them too hard at this stage. I figure we'll bed the herd down and cross first thing in the morning. Tomorrow we'll hold them in Sundance Hollow where Bill suggested and give the crew a break in town. It will also give me an opportunity to see if I can pick up any more riders.'

'A good idea,' agreed Dan.

The three men parted and when Dan reached his office in Red Springs he found Clint Schofield still there.

'Mason hasn't moved from the Silver Dollar,' Clint informed him.

Dan nodded, but did not answer. He looked thoughtful for a few moments before speaking. 'Clint,' he said, 'I'm going to play a hunch. It looks to me as if Mason might be waiting for someone. I'd like to see how the news about the herd affects him. I want you to go over to the Silver Dollar and make it known casually that O'Grady is not going to cross the Brazo until tomorrow.' Dan smiled when he saw the mystified look on his deputy's face. 'Just make sure Mason hears it,' he added.

Clint nodded and, picking up his Stetson, left the office, crossed the street and pushed his way through the squeaking batwings. He paused just inside the saloon, and then ambled over to the long, mahogany counter against which he had noticed Butch Mason was leaning.

'Beer, Joe, please.' When the man brought the drink Clint said, 'Reckon you'll hev a busy day tomorrow.'

'How come?' asked Joe. 'Thought the

trail-herders would be in tonight.'

'O'Grady's holding his herd on the south side of the Brazo until tomorrow,' explained Clint. 'He's had several of his outfit killed by rustlers and he figures being short-handed he wouldn't get across before darkness. Once the herd is across Bill Collins is going to let two of his men help O'Grady's ramrod to watch it to give the drovers a long spell in town.'

'Thet sure suits me,' grinned Joe.

Clint knew that Butch Mason could not have failed to hear this news. The gunman finished his drink and strolled casually from the saloon. Clint waited until Mason had passed through the batwings, then crossed to the window, from where he saw Mason untie his horse and lead it to the hotel. Mason hitched his horse to the rail and, when he had gone inside the building, Clint hurried across the street to the sheriff's office.

Dan was surprised at the way Mason had reacted to the news. 'I didn't expect him to book in at the hotel,' he said. 'Wonder if my hunch was wrong.' He paused thoughtfully. 'Clint, will you keep an eye on Mason? I'll ride down to the ford in the morning, straight from home, and keep an eye on the crossing. I still think Mason may try something down there. Be sure to tail him when he leaves the hotel in the morning.'

Clint nodded and Dan picked up his sombrero, left the office and, in the gathering darkness, rode out of Red Springs in the direction of his ranch.

Clint stared thoughtfully after him from the window. 'Mason may move before morning,' he muttered to himself. 'I guess I'll keep an eye on the hotel until I know he's settled for the night.'

The deputy left the office and strolled casually along the sidewalk. Mason's horse was still outside the hotel and this puzzled Clint. If Mason intended staying in Red Springs why hadn't he taken the animal to the livery stable? If he meant to ride away why had he gone into the hotel? Clint entered the building and strolled across to the desk, where the clerk greeted him pleasantly.

'Don't suppose you're looking for a room,' he grinned. 'What can I do for you?'

'Butch Mason came in here a short while ago,' replied Clint. 'How long is he staying?'

'Booked in for one night,' answered the clerk.

'Thanks,' said Clint, and left the hotel unaware that his brief conversation had been

64

overheard by Mason who, on hearing his name mentioned, had paused at the top of the stairs.

When he heard the front door of the hotel close, Mason hurried down the stairs determined to find out who had been making enquiries about him. He paused momentarily outside the hotel, but it gave him time to recognise the figure of the deputy sheriff leaning on a railing a short distance along the sidewalk. Mason's eyes narrowed; so the law was keeping an eye on him; he would have to get rid of the tin-star. He turned along the sidewalk, and, as he walked briskly, his mind quickly formulated a plan. He recalled that on the first day he had ridden into Red Springs he had noticed two broken-down shacks on the edge of town, and, now, as the darkness was filling the Texas sky, Mason headed for these buildings.

As soon as Clint estimated that Mason was far enough ahead of him to follow without raising suspicion, he pushed himself from the railings and headed in the same direction. Mason's pace was brisk, and Clint reckoned that he must have some prearranged plan, maybe a meeting. The deputy was surprised when Mason kept on walking when he reached the end of Main Street. There were only two dilapidated shacks ahead. Suddenly Clint's thoughts raced. Was one of them to be used as a meeting place? Could he be on the verge of an important discovery? Excitedly, Clint closed the distance between himself and the man ahead. He could not afford to lose sight of him in the darkness. As Mason neared the hut, Clint slowed his pace. When he saw Mason enter the doorless hut Clint hurried swiftly but silently forward. He must reach the broken window to overhear what was said in order to identify Mason's mysterious contact.

Once inside the hut Butch Mason flattened himself against the wall beside the door-post. He smiled to himself as he drew his Colt; the prying lawman was due for a shock. The gunman tensed himself, listening to the almost silent movement of the deputy. He realised Clint was making for the window and, when the movement stopped, Mason slid silently round the door-post keyed for instant action. As he came into the open he saw the figure of Clint with his back to him pressed close to the wall beside the window. Two swift strides carried Mason forward and, before Clint could turn, a Colt slashed across the back of his head and he slumped to the floor in a silent heap.

Mason reholstered his Colt and grinned as he knelt beside the unconscious deputy.

He untied Clint's neckerchief and gagged him tightly. He dragged him inside the hut, drew the unconscious man's Colt from its holster and threw it into one corner. Mason left the hut and hurried back to town where he mounted his horse, and returned quickly to the hut. Clint was soon secured with Mason's lariat. Satisfied that the deputy would not be free for a considerable time, Mason remounted his horse and headed in a southerly direction.

The following morning Dan McCoy was up early and, after checking with his foreman that there were no problems at the ranch, he said goodbye to his wife and headed for Wayman's Ford. Shaun O'Grady was already on the move and the first cattle were already in the water. The swollen river was flowing fast, but the drovers handled the bellowing steers skillfully and the complete herd was taken across the river without mishap. Throughout the operation Dan had kept a ceaseless watch for anything unusual. He saw no strangers, nor anyone acting suspiciously. He had half expected Clint to report to him about Mason, but was somewhat relieved when he did not do so. He must have been wrong about the intentions of the gunman; if there had been the slightest suspicion about his actions Dan knew that Clint would have reported to him.

Once the herd was safely across the Brazo and on its way to Sundance Hollow, Dan returned to Red Springs. He knew it would not be long before the drovers rode into town for a well earned relaxation once Bill Collins's two cowboys had joined O'Grady's ramrod in watching the herd. When he reached his office Dan was surprised to find that Clint was not there, but he was even more surprised that there was no note for him from his deputy. Whatever Mason's actions were, Clint must be keeping a close watch on him. However, Dan decided to check on Mason himself and left his office for the hotel.

'Howdy, Dan,' greeted the clerk as the sheriff crossed the hotel lobby.

Dan returned the greeting. 'Has Mason checked out yet?' he asked.

'This morning,' replied the clerk.

'Didn't say where he was heading by any chance?' queried Dan.

'No,' came the answer. 'Just paid his bill and left.'

'Thanks,' said Dan and returned to his office. There was nothing he could do but await the return of his deputy.

About an hour later the pound of hooves and the shouts of men indicated the arrival of the drovers bent on enjoying their break from the monotonous, hard, lonely life of trailing a herd to the railheads in Kansas. Dan crossed to the window and watched them pull to a halt outside the Silver Dollar and follow Shaun O'Grady through the batwings.

As the drovers thronged to the bar and lined themselves along the mahogany counter, saloon girls laughing and shouting greetings joined them. Soon beer was flowing freely and the whole saloon was alive with noise. The whole proceedings were being watched with some amusement by a short, stocky, broad shouldered man whose dark, cold eyes kept straying to Shaun O'Grady. The moment Mason had been waiting for was getting close.

After about half an hour O'Grady noticed a poker game was about to begin at one of the tables, and he moved across to join the other players. As he sat down Mason pulled up a chair on the opposite side of the table. The game started and everything proceeded normally with O'Grady winning and Mason on the losing end. When it came to Mason's turn to deal he shuffled the cards deftly making sure he left two high cards on the bottom of the pack. He noticed O'Grady was watching him, but the other players were not attentive to his dealing.

'Hold it,' O'Grady's voice rapped harshly.

Mason froze in his deal. The other men looked up sharply.

'You've just dealt yourself off the bottom,' accused the trail boss. Mason's dark eyes narrowed.

'You're a liar!' he hissed venomously.

O'Grady grabbed for Mason's cards and the gunman purposely moved them that fraction slower so that O'Grady got there first. Shaun flung them face upwards on the table. It was a good hand. His eyes were smouldering angrily as he looked straight at Mason.

'Am I still a liar?' he demanded harshly.

'You are,' lashed back Mason. 'That proved nothing.' He glanced at the other players. 'Anyone else see me deal off the bottom?'

The men shook their heads, mumbling their replies in the negative.

'I saw you!' called O'Grady.

A silence had gradually descended on the whole saloon and a violent tension seemed to spark across the table between the two men. The situation was building up as Mason had hoped; it would not take much more to provoke O'Grady.

'You're still a liar!' The words lashed into the cattleman's brain.

He pushed himself slowly from the table and Mason, dropping the remaining cards on the table, matched O'Grady's movement. The other players realising what was coming hastily scrambled away from their chairs.

'No man calls me a liar.' O'Grady's voice was quiet but full of menace.

'I do.' Mason's voice was cold and accusing.

O'Grady's hand moved upwards to his side with the speed of a snake, but even as his Colt cleared his leather Mason's gun roared. An incredulous look crossed the cattleman's face as he staggered backwards under the impact of the bullet in his stomach. His chair slithered with him and, as his knees buckled, he slumped down on to the seat before doubling up and pitching forward against the table, a fixed glassy stare in his eyes.

The shock of the gunfire had come so suddenly that the whole saloon was stunned into immobility. It was only for a few moments, but Mason used that time. He moved swiftly towards the door, keeping a menacing Colt covering the occupants of the saloon.

'Keep your hands away from your guns,'

rapped Mason loudly. There was no mistaking his intentions should anyone be foolhardy enough to try to draw on Butch Mason.

ıHe was near the batwings when the sheriff, who had heard the shots from his office, burst in with a Colt in his hand. His steel blue eyes sized up the situation in a flash. 'Hold it, Mason,' he snapped. O'Grady's dead! Another trail boss killed! Mason was the killer! Mason here! Where was Clint? What had been happening? Dan's thoughts raced.

'Self-defence,' said Mason. 'He drew on me first.'

'Is that so?' Dan glanced round the occupants of the saloon and received glum nods from most people. There was not one protestation against Mason's statement. He looked at Mason. 'Holster your gun,' he said coldly. 'If I were you I'd get out of here as soon as possible.'

Mason grinned as he slipped his Colt back into its leather. 'Is that a threat or advice?' he said smoothly. He shrugged his shoulders. 'No matter, I am riding.' He swung on his heels and pushed through the batwings.

Immediately the drovers plunged forward threatening to get Mason, but they found themselves halted by the cold muzzle of

Dan's threatening Colt. They protested loudly.

'You're shielding a killer!'

'Get out of my way, Sheriff!'

'He wants stringing up!'

'Quiet! Quiet!' yelled Dan. 'You all admitted it was self-defence. No one came forward to say otherwise. If O'Grady drew first there is nothing I can do.'

'He was deliberately provoked,' yelled one of the drovers.

'Mason certainly goaded O'Grady on,' said one of the card-players.

'Seemed to me he deliberately set out to make O'Grady draw first,' said another.

'Even so,' replied Dan, 'if O'Grady drew first Mason killed him in self-defence.' This was typical of Mason's work; a trust in his fast draw to kill the man he wanted and keep on the right side of the law. He was somewhat relieved when he heard a horse galloping along Main Street and a quick glance out of the window told him Butch Mason was leaving Red Springs at all possible speed.

The bunch of drovers stirred uneasily, murmuring loudly against Dan; angry that the killer should be getting away under the protection of the law, but there was nothing they could do against the ever watchful sheriff who barred their path with his Colt.

'Just simmer down,' called Dan. 'Believe me, I regret this happened, but I'll have no revenge killing. You can leave shortly.'

The drovers turned away, still gathered in a small threatening group. Dan stood by the batwings, watching the cowboys carefully. He felt sure that Mason had returned to Red Springs for the purpose of killing O'Grady. But what had happened to Clint? Why hadn't he still been keeping an eye on Mason? Dan felt concerned for the well-being of his deputy.

Ten minutes passed before Dan spoke again. 'You can go now,' he announced, addressing the drovers. He reckoned he had given Mason enough time to prevent the drovers from following him. As much as he disapproved of Mason, Dan did not want to have a lynching on his hands as well. The drovers moved outside taking the body of their trail boss with them. Dan watched them from the sidewalk and when they were all mounted, one man glared hard at the sheriff.

'We'll be back and Red Springs had better watch out,' he shouted. 'Our ramrod will not take this lying down and we'll back him.'

Before Dan could warn them against any foolhardy action the drovers pulled their horses round and thundered out of Red Springs. Dan stared after them, his mind toying with the possibility behind the threat. Whatever he did he must protect the town. He turned back into the saloon.

'It looks as if we might have trouble from the drovers,' he called. 'I'd like volunteers to prevent them from shooting up the town.' Ten men stepped forward offering their services, and Dan eyed them shrewdly. 'It might come to a gun-fight,' he went on. 'I won't blame anyone who wants to back down.' He paused, but no one moved. 'Thanks,' said Dan gratefully. 'I reckon we'd better ride about a mile out along the south trail; there are plenty of boulders around there to give us protection should we have a gun-fight. Anyone without a rifle can get one from my office now.'

A group of men followed Dan from the Silver Dollar. They were half-way across the street when Dan stopped in his tracks. The dishevelled figure of his deputy was hurrying along the sidewalk. Dan could see at a glance there had been trouble, and he hurried to meet Clint.

'What on earth happened to you?' asked Dan when he reached the older man.

There was anger and annoyance written all

over Clint's face. 'That low-down, no-good Mason out-smarted me,' he said viciously, and went on to tell Dan what had happened.

'Are you sure he met no one at the shack?' asked Dan when Clint had finished his story.

'I couldn't be certain,' said Clint, 'but I was jumped so soon after reaching the shack that I figure he must have known I was following him. I reckon he lured me out there so he could get me out of the way.'

'He succeeded in doing that all right,' replied Dan grimly, and went on to tell Clint of the shooting. 'It looks as if we'll have trouble with the drovers. We're just on our way to stop them getting back into town.'

The two men walked to the sheriff's office, where Clint cleaned himself up whilst Dan issued rifles to the ten men.

'Get your horses,' he instructed. 'I'll be ready in five minutes.'

When the men had left the office Dan turned to Clint. 'Are you all right?' he asked.

Clint nodded. 'I'd sure like to get my hands on Butch Mason.'

'You'd better get yourself a meal,' said Dan, 'then join us.'

'Suits me,' said the deputy. 'It seems to me that Mason deliberately set out to get

O'Grady. Somehow he knew I was following him so got me out of the way, but how could he be certain the drovers would be in town this morning?'

'Remember he overheard you tell the barman last night,' pointed out Dan. 'It was almost certain that O'Grady would come into Red Springs as soon as the herd was bedded down. It was Mason's reaction to this information that I wanted to know.'

'Sorry if I let you down, Dan,' apologised Clint.

'Don't worry about that,' replied Dan. 'It couldn't be helped, but I'd like to know what Mason did after he knocked you out.'

Glancing out of the window, the sheriff saw that his posse was ready.

'See you later, Clint,' he said and hurried outside to his horse.

Dan was thoughtful throughout the ride, but he would have been alarmed if he had known that, at the moment the posse were taking up their positions a mile out of Red Springs, Butch Mason was greeting Sam Brady at a point overlooking the late Shaun O'Grady's herd.

5

Sam Brady looked questioningly at Butch Mason as he swung from the saddle.

'Everything go all right?' he asked anxiously.

'Sure,' drawled Butch casually. 'Butch Mason never fails.'

A grin broke across Sam Brady's face; he slapped Mason on the shoulder. 'Good work, Butch, good work,' he praised. 'Two of them have got what they deserve.' There was a deep note of satisfaction in his voice. He was pleased with the way his plans were going and was glad that he had hired Mason for this particular job. 'Were the drovers riled up about it?' he asked.

Mason grinned. 'They sure were. McCoy had the drop on them, but they were in an ugly mood. I figure he'll see that they leave town but he won't be able to stop them going back. I reckon they'll come back here; they lack a leader at the moment, but with their ramrod at their head Red Springs and Dan McCoy can look out.'

'I hope you're right,' said Brady. 'If that happens it will leave only two Bar X cowboys with the herd; it's goin' to be easy to take the lot. Your trip back to the ranch last night after laying that deputy out, sure saved us an all-night watch.'

'You by-passed the herd without being seen?' asked Mason.

'Yes,' replied Brady. 'We were in the saddle early and across Wayman's Ford before first light.'

'Good,' replied Mason. He paused thoughtfully, then as he continued, a note of caution came into his voice. 'I still think we'd better be leaving the herd alone now that it is across the Brazo. If we take it here it means that we have to recross the river, and we can't use Wayman's Ford; it's near to the Bar X and Red Springs.'

'We'll drive the cattle eastwards along the river and cross lower down,' pointed out Brady.

'That may be difficult the way the river is running, and we're sure to be followed in daylight,' pointed out Mason.

'If things go the way you say, those drovers and McCoy are going to be so tied up that we'll be away to the east and across the Brazo before they get after us,' said Brady.

'I don't like it,' said Mason doubtfully. 'My advice to you is…'

Brady stiffened. 'Mason!' he cut in abruptly, a note of annoyance in his voice. 'When I want your advice I'll ask for it. I'm running the show, you are merely a hired-gun; I'm paying the money so I'll call the tune. See that it stays that way.'

Mason stared at Brady in amazement; words sprang to his lips but he stifled them. Brady was paying him good money; maybe it was best left that way. He turned to his horse and led it to the others grouped in the hollow. Brady watched him for a moment then climbed the slope until he reached a man who was sitting amongst a group of boulders at one end of the rise.

'We figure that the drovers shouldn't be long now if all goes as we hope,' he told the man. 'Give me the signal as soon as you see them.'

The man nodded, and Brady clambered back down the slope to rejoin his men. He waited impatiently, nervously dragging at a cheroot whilst he paced up and down. Every few minutes he glanced in the direction of the boulders hoping for the signal. Twenty minutes passed, and Brady was beginning to think that their estimations had been incorrect, when he saw the man wave his rifle. Brady snatched the cheroot from his mouth, threw it away and hurried to join the cowboy. Mason saw Brady start off up the slope and raced after him. When they reached the look-out, he pointed to a group of riders moving at a steady trot towards a second hollow about a quarter of a mile away to their right. The three men watched in silence until the riders dropped out of sight.

'Come on, Mason. We'll take a closer look,' said Brady, pushing himself to his feet.

The two men made use of the cover offered by the boulders which were strewn between the two hollows. When they neared the rim of the second hollow the two men dropped to their stomachs and crept forward until the herd came into view. The second hollow was much bigger than that in which Brady's men were laid up, and below them the herd was grazing peacefully.

There was much activity among the drovers and everyone appeared to be saying something to the ramrod at once. From their shouts and gesticulations Brady could see that the men were in an ugly, angry mood. A few moments passed, then the group of men hurried to the wagon, and Brady and Mason saw rifles being issued to the drovers.

'Looks as if we guessed right,' grinned Brady, with a note of satisfaction in his voice.

Mason nodded unsmilingly; he still had doubts about the wisdom of this attack. When he had reported to Brady last night he had tried to persuade him not to go through with the rustling, but Brady had insisted. Mason realised he had nothing to do but play along; after all, his pay was high and after two more killings his task would be over.

As soon as the drovers were armed they hurried to their horses. Brady saw one of them have a brief word with two men, and when these two men were left behind he knew they must be the Bar X riders. Once into the saddles the horses were kicked into a gallop and they thundered out of the hollow in the direction of Red Springs.

'C'm on,' called Brady. 'We've got to act fast and get as much ground under our feet as quickly as possible.'

Brady and Mason ran back to their men and, after a brief word of instruction, Brady led the rustlers towards the herd. When they broke into the hollow at an earth-pounding gallop the rustlers were strung out in a long line so that they hit the herd on a broad front. Taken completely by surprise, the two Bar X men did not have time to draw their guns before they were sent spinning from their saddles by the guns of two of the rustlers.

Frightened by the sudden onslaught of the yelling men, the steers turned, pushing one against the other, to get away from the noise. The movement rippled across the herd until the steers on the far side were forced to turn and run. With this easing of the pressure the whole herd moved in a mass after the leaders. Steers bellowed; horns pressed against horns and ripped into flesh; dust rose under the earth-tearing hooves as the cattle broke into a run. Riders quickly ranged along the side of the herd, keeping it compact as instructed by Brady. Others had raced ahead and were soon controlling the pace of the herd as the urging of the rustlers at the rear eased. Whatever happened they must keep the herd moving at a fast pace, but they had to be careful that a stampede did not break out.

The cattle moved swiftly out of the hollow, which by this time was filled with choking dust, and moved across the grassland on a track parallel to the river. As he broke out of the hollow, Brady glanced across the countryside in the direction of Red Springs. There was no sign of the drovers, and Brady complimented himself on the timing of the raid; the drovers had not heard the gun-shots nor the disturbance. Now, if all went well, they could be well to the east and across the Brazo before the drovers found their cattle were missing. He settled himself in the saddle to keep an eye on the general situation and, at the same time, found comfort in the fact that Butch Mason was hanging back, as planned, to keep watch for sign of pursuit.

Sam Brady would not have felt so easy in his mind if he had known that at that moment the figure of a cowboy stirred in the settling dust in the hollow. Consciousness came slowly to the Bar X cowboy, Sloane Jenkins. As some sort of reason burned its way back into his brain he was aware of a sharp pain high in his chest, just below his right shoulder. He struggled to sit up, wincing with the pain of the effort. He sank back to the ground, gasping for breath. His brain cleared and he was suddenly aware of what had happened. Alarm seized him. The herd had gone! He must warn someone as soon as possible. Sloane struggled to get up once more, and this time, spurred on by the urgency of the situation, he was successful. He stood for a few moments swaying on his feet. At all costs he must keep upright; his shoulder hurt, and, glancing down, Sloane winced at the ugly-looking wound from which the blood was flowing freely. He looked around for his horse, but the animal was not to be seen. Sloane guessed it must have run with the cattle and, with regret at the delay this would bring, he started to walk in the direction of the Bar X ranch. The cowboy struggled up the slope. Every second's delay was enabling the rustlers to get further away. Sloane reckoned they would think he was dead; if only he could get help quickly the rustlers would be in for a big surprise.

Reaching the top of the rise, Sloane paused, gasping for breath. His shoulder throbbed. Sweat poured from him and his head spun. The sun felt unbearably hot. Suddenly he stiffened with excitement. A smile twisted across his pain-drawn face. His horse stood champing at some grass a short distance away. Sloane's brain pounded. In his weak state, was he imagining things or had his horse been passed by the rush of the rustlers and sought safety behind them?

Sloane started forward eagerly, and the sudden movement caused the horse to look up. Recognising the cowboy, it whinneyed affectionately and moved towards him. When he reached the horse the wounded man grasped the saddle for support, then with considerable effort managed to drag himself into it. He tapped the horse with his heels sending it towards the Bar X as he slumped forward in the saddle.

ǀBill Collins was watching the Bar X men breaking in horses in the corrals near the ranch-house. The work was going smoothly when one of the men drew Bill's attention to the lone rider approaching the ranch at slow pace.

'Things don't seem to be right with that hombre,' said the cowboy.

Bill's eyes narrowed against the glare of the sun. 'They sure don't,' he muttered and swung from the corral fence on which he had been sitting.

He hurried to his horse which was tied to the rail in front of the house and, once in the saddle, put the animal into a gallop towards the lone rider. He had not gone far when he received a shock on recognising Sloane Jenkins. Bill pushed his horse faster and was soon bringing his animal alongside Sloane. The cowboy raised his head and smiled weakly at his boss.

'Mr Collins,' he gasped, 'the herd's gone.'

'What!' Bill was shaken by the news, but, recognising his immediate duty towards his cowboy, he turned his attention to Sloane.

'You've caught a bad one there,' he said, indicating his shoulder. 'We'll soon have you back and get the doctor for you.'

'Reckon those hombres thought I was dead...' Sloane's words came out with great effort.

'Don't talk now,' instructed Bill. 'We'll soon be back.'

The Bar X men watched the riders approach and, as soon as they saw Sloane's condition, they hurried to help. Strong, firm hands lifted him from the saddle and carried him into the bunkhouse. Bill Collins issued orders quickly and crisply. A cowboy was sent to town for the doctor whilst two men were ordered to saddle everyone's horses.

'What's happened?' asked his foreman.

'Don't know the full story,' replied Collins. 'Sloane said the herd had been rustled and the gang must have thought him dead. We're going to need these horses. Let's see if we can find out any more from him.'

The two men entered the bunkhouse to find that two men were already making Sloane more comfortable and that he seemed a little more conscious of his surroundings.

'I've sent for the doc,' said Bill. 'Feel like talking?'

Sloane nodded. 'The drovers returned from Red Springs with the body of Shaun O'Grady.'

'What!' Bill gasped. This was something completely unexpected.

'Butch Mason killed him,' went on Sloane. 'The drovers were riled up because the sheriff seemed to have backed Mason up because it was self-defence. They came back for the ramrod and have ridden to have it out with the sheriff.'

There was alarm in their eyes as Bill Collins and his foreman exchanged glances.

Sloane drew a deep breath from which he seemed to find energy to continue. 'A short while after they had gone this gang hit us hard; we hadn't a chance it happened so quickly. I figure they must have thought I was dead. If I had been they would have got clean away.'

'Recognise any of them?' asked Bill grimly.

'No,' replied the cowboy, 'they were all masked. They headed east along the Brazo; you'll be able to catch up with them.'

'Right,' answered Collins and walked outside, followed by his foreman.

'What are we going to do?' asked the foreman. 'Hadn't we better help the sheriff?' There was an urgent note in his voice. 'After all, the cattle aren't really our responsibility.'

'Maybe not,' replied Collins, 'but rustlers are the responsibility of any cattlemen. At any rate, both things may be tied up together. It seems strange that the rustlers should be on the spot when the drovers were absent. It looks as if they had anticipated or even knew what was going to happen. I think those drovers probably threatened Dan before they rode out of town and Dan will have taken precautions; he'll be all right. If we get after the rustlers we might be able to put an end to the whole affair.'

Bill Collins called his cowboys and instructed one to remain with Sloane whilst another was ordered to ride to Red Springs to contact the drovers and the sheriff. The rest of the Bar X outfit were soon mounted and leaving the ranch in an easterly direction, at a thundering gallop.

Once he was satisfied that the men from Red Springs were strategically situated behind the boulders Dan moved closer to the trail. The men relaxed, knowing there would be some time to wait before anything developed. Dan waited impatiently. This sort of speculative waiting annoyed him, especially when there were more important things that could do with his attention. The drovers may not return, common sense may have prevailed, the ramrod of the outfit may have seen that it would be senseless to ride against Red Springs, but Dan doubted it. The drovers were in an ugly mood when they had left town, and he didn't expect their ramrod would take O'Grady's killing without protest. How he wished he could have followed Mason; maybe he would have found the answer to a number of questions which troubled him. What was Mason's connection with Sam Brady, if any? Was there any link between Mason and the rustlers? Were the killings of Matt Stevens and Shaun O'Grady both performed by the same man? If so, why had Mason gone after the trail bosses? Would he strike at Burt Pallister and Seth Cunliffe who were still pushing herds towards the Brazo?

Dan's thoughts were interrupted by the sound of a horse approaching from Red Springs. He drew his Colt from his holster, but relaxed when he saw the rider was Clint Schofield. Dan returned his gun to the leather and went to meet Clint as he pulled his horse to a halt.

'How are you feeling, Clint?' asked Dan.

'I'm all right,' replied the deputy. 'Any

chance of getting on Mason's trail? I'd sure like to git that hombre.'

'You aren't likely to be able to trace him now,' replied Dan. 'I guess he's probably ridden back to the hills.' He halted the suggestion which sprang to Clint's lips. 'And you aren't riding that way now. Stay here with us; we may need an extra gun.'

'I sure hope it doesn't come to that with these drovers,' said Clint grimly.

'It won't if I have anything to do with it,' said Dan.

The two men were discussing recent events when the dull pound of distant galloping horses brought their conversation to a stop.

'This could be the drovers,' called out Dan. He saw the men from Red Springs ease their rifles on the boulders. Stepping on to the trail, he walked a short distance ahead of the line of men. Clint followed and the lawmen waited grimly as the pounding grew louder and louder. When the drovers appeared over a rise in the trail, a short distance ahead, he loosed off a shot into the sky.

The drovers hauled on their reins and brought their horses to a milling halt a short distance from the lawmen. They eyed Dan's Colt with a mixture of surprise and annoyance. Dust swirled under the trampling hooves as the cowboys held their horses in an uneasy check. A man stabbed his horse forward from the group and approached Dan. He halted the animal in front of the lawman and glared angrily at him.

'That tin star isn't goin' to prevent us hitting Red Springs for the death of Shaun O'Grady,' he snapped. 'An' you are coming back with us.'

'Maybe the star won't stop you losing your heads,' replied Dan sharply, 'but the rifles that are covering your outfit will.' He had raised his voice so that all the drovers could hear him. 'My advice to you is to forget the whole thing and concentrate on getting that herd to the rail-head safely. That's the way Shaun would want it.'

'O'Grady was killed by a renowned gun-man. We blame Red Springs for allowing him to be there and then letting him get away,' rapped back the ramrod.

'Hold hard,' shouted Dan. 'I know Mason's reputation and I was having him watched, but something went wrong. Apart from that Mason lived up to his reputation; your boss was killed in self-defence; your drovers agreed with this when I made that point in the Silver Dollar. The result is that the law could do nothing about Mason, except protect him from men who were prepared to break the law by lynching him. As mean and disreputable as he is, Mason was entitled to that protection. At the same time I protected the drovers; if they'd lynched Mason every one of them would have been a murderer and they would be at the mercy of the law now.'

'What I hear,' replied the ramrod testily, 'O'Grady was provoked into drawing first and in our book provoking a man like that is as good as murdering him.'

'Mason stood the chance of being killed,' answered Dan. 'He didn't know if O'Grady was fast with a gun or not.'

'Makes no difference, Sheriff,' rapped the ramrod. 'Call your men off and we'll do what we have to do without anyone gettin' hurt; if you don't then we'll sure have to ride over you to get into Red Springs because one thing is certain, that town is not going to forget our boss was killed there.'

Dan saw it was useless to argue any more. The events had warped the drovers' minds so that they could see no sense in the law. 'You aren't passing us!' he replied grimly. The ramrod said nothing but pulled his horse round sharply and rode back to the group of impatient drovers.

As soon as he moved, Dan and Clint hurried back to the cover of the boulders. The drovers scattered quickly, seeking cover, and both sides exchanged a few tentative shots. Gradually the firing died down as both sides realised that it was going to be a question of one outsmarting the other. Eyes kept close watch for any movement, trying to detect any sign of an attempt to outflank each other. The afternoon wore on, the odd bullet whined across the intervening space without causing any damage. Dan realised that the longer they waited the more chance there was of the drovers calming down and seeing reason.

Suddenly the sound of hoofbeats heralded the approach of a rider behind the drovers. When he topped the rise and saw the drovers, with rifles at the ready, behind cover, the Bar X cowboy pulled the horse to a halt. He realised the situation in a flash and knew that Bill Collins had surmised correctly when he had reckoned Dan would be prepared for the arrival of the drovers. Somewhere hidden by boulders were the sheriff and men from Red Springs.

'Hold it,' yelled the cowboy at the top of his voice. 'I'm from the Bar X; I have some bad news for the sheriff and you drovers.'

There was an urgent note in his voice, and from the tone no one doubted his word. The drovers and the men from Red Springs broke cover simultaneously. All thought of their fight had been driven from their minds by the lone horseman who now rode towards them.

By the time Dan reached him the drovers were clamouring around him. The cowboy nodded to Dan. 'Bill Collins told me to contact you and the ramrod, to tell you the herd has been rustled!'

'What!' There was a gasp from the men crowding round. Everyone suddenly started talking at once.

'Quiet!' yelled Dan. 'Let's hear what happened.'

When the noise subsided the cowboy told the story of the attack on the herd. As it unfolded, Dan's thoughts raced and, when the cowboy finished speaking, Dan turned to the ramrod.

'Looks to me as though those rustlers were expecting you to leave the herd,' he said.

The ramrod nodded grimly. 'Then the killing was a put-up job to get us away from the herd.'

'Well, to a certain extent, yes,' replied Dan,

'but I figure there was more to it than that. Mason was out to get O'Grady for some other reason, but the rustlers saw a good opportunity to use it, expecting you would be mad enough to try to take it out on Red Springs and leave the herd weakly guarded.'

'Seems we played right into their hands,' muttered the ramrod dejectedly. 'Sorry for what we've done.'

Dan sympathised with him. 'The rustlers won't get far,' he reassured him. 'The Bar X outfit are after them and if the rustlers are expecting to cross the Brazo they will find themselves up against it. C'm on, we'd better ride.'

Drovers and cowboys raced to their horses and were soon riding for the Brazo.

6

Sam Brady was pleased with the way things were going. The cattle were moving at a quick pace and a stampede, which might easily have developed in the early stages of the raid, had been prevented. He was glad he had brought in these Kansas cowboys to handle the rustling side of his schemes. Satisfied that everything was under control, he rode to a cowboy on the right flank of the herd.

'Jake,' he called as he pulled alongside. 'We'll ride ahead and look for a place to cross the Brazo.'

'Right,' called Jake, and both men pushed their mounts into a gallop and gradually outrode the herd.

For five miles they rode close to the river bank without finding a suitable place to put the cattle across. Brady was beginning to get a little worried. He wanted these cattle on the south side of the Brazo as soon as possible so that he could make for the hills. He thought it would be some time before the drovers returned and the raid was discovered, but he couldn't be certain; Sheriff McCoy was clever and if he persuaded the drovers to forget their revenge they might be back soon. The Brazo was running higher than he had expected and he regretted the delay in finding a place to cross. Impatiently he pushed his horse a little faster.

'This looks a likely place,' said Brady, when they reached a wider part of the river where water swirled less swiftly.

The two men pulled to a halt. Jake weighed up the situation carefully.

'Wouldn't advise it, Mr Brady,' he said.

'But the river's not flowing as fast here,' protested Brady.

'Maybe not, but it is too deep and there are one or two tricky currents by the look of it,' replied Jake.

'We've got to get across,' said Brady irritably. 'I think we could do it.'

Jake shrugged his shoulders. 'Whatever you say,' he drawled. 'You're the boss but I wouldn't advise it.' Brady's face clouded with anger; he hated being told anything especially by people he had hired, even though they had more experience than he. He pulled his horse round sharply and kicked it forward. Jake followed and the two men rode for another mile.

'Looks as though there has been a ford here,' said Jake, indicting the slope on the bank a short distance ahead.

The two men stopped close to the water and viewed the crossing.

'Well?' snapped Brady irritably when Jake made no comment.

'It might be possible here,' replied Jake. 'It will be risky but if we are pushed we could give it a try.'

'Pushed? Of course we are pushed,' said Brady testily. 'We want to be across the

Brazo as soon as possible. I'd hoped to be heading to the hills by now. We'll have to chance this crossing.'

The two men pulled their horses round and kicked them into a gallop towards the herd. When they reached it, Brady worked his way along one side of the herd issuing instructions about the crossing to the men, whilst Jake did the same on the other side. They were talking to the men riding drag when Jake let out a yell.

'Trouble!' He pointed in the direction of a horseman who was tearing across the ground at an earth-pounding gallop.

'Mason!' said Brady and he and Jake stabbed their horses forward to meet him.

The hired killer hauled on the reins as Brady and Jake turned to meet him.

'They're on to us,' he yelled. 'The Bar X outfit. One of those hombres can't have been dead and must have got back.'

Alarm showed on Brady's face. He glanced back; there was no sign of their pursuers, but once they topped that last rise they would be in sight.

'Can we make that old ford?' asked Jake.

'Forget that,' replied Brady. 'We'll use that first place, where the river was wider.'

'We'll never get across there,' called Jake,

alarm showing in his voice. 'We'd better make a run for that old ford.'

'We'll take the river where I said,' snapped Brady. 'It's not as bad as you make it out to be. We must get across before the Bar X men reach us, then we can hold them off from the other side, but if we make for the old ford the extra distance will give them more time to catch up to us.'

'If those cattle resist at the…,' started Jake.

Brady's eyes blazed furiously. 'Don't argue,' he snapped. 'Just get on with the job and stop wasting time with your objections.' He kicked his horse into a gallop and, after an exchange of glances, Mason and Jake followed suit. When they reached the herd Brady and Jake yelled orders quickly and the steers turned towards the Brazo. The cowboys riding drag shouted loudly, urging the cattle faster, whilst the point men, forcing the lead steers onwards, also endeavoured to keep the front line compact. Mason hung back watching the horizon for the first sight of the Bar X men as they broke over the rise in the ground.

The first cattle tried to slow at the sight of the water, but, forced on by the pressure of the cattle behind them, they plunged bellowing into the river. Two cowboys went with them to lead them across, but immediately they sensed the danger which lay in this crossing. The river was running so high that almost immediately on entering the water the cattle and horses were forced to swim. One of the cowboys yelled to those still on the bank, but his words of warning were lost in the noise of the bellowing steers which milled on the bank. Dust rose in a great cloud churned up by the tearing hooves. Cattle crashed against cattle and cowboys cursed and swore trying to drive the steers into the water. Some of the herd broke away and thundered along the bank of the river. Brady yelled to his men to let them go and get what cattle they could into the water. The first cattle were a quarter of the way across when Mason galloped up with the information that they had been sighted by the Bar X outfit.

Brady cursed loudly at the news. He rode everywhere, forcing steers into the water, urging his men in their task. Jake glanced anxiously in the direction of the approaching posse then galloped over to Brady.

'Better get ourselves across,' he yelled. 'We won't get many more cattle into the water before they're on us.'

Brady's face was clouded with anger at the

turn of events against him, but a searching look across the grassland told him that Jake was right.

'Right,' he agreed and yelled to his men. 'Let them go! Get yourselves across!'

The first bunch of cattle were about half-way across when suddenly some of them floundered and, met by a stronger current, were swept down-stream, frightened by the extra thrust of the water. Steers tried to turn to seek the safety of the bank they had just left. Pandemonium reigned in the water and cattle thrust and struggled against the tugging water. They buffeted one against the other; fear gripped them, and as their strength was overcome by the river, steer after steer was swept away in the swirling waters. Those that regained the bank only added to the confusion there, but once the pressure of the cowboys ceased, after Brady's order, the cattle stampeded away from the terror to which they had been driven.

Brady halted his horse on the river bank. He shouted and waved his men to get across the Brazo, ordered them not to stop to fight. If anyone was caught the identity of the brains behind the killing and the rustling would be in jeopardy. Brady was annoyed the way things had turned out this time, but this was only a minor set-back. There were still two more herds heading north, and these were to be dealt with. Provided everyone got across the Brazo, Brady felt convinced that no one would be any wiser about him and he would be free to attack the other herds as planned. He kept an anxious eye on the fast-approaching Bar X men as he watched his men take to the swiftly flowing river.

Sensing that they were going to lose the rustlers, Bill Collins and his cowboys opened fire. Their only hope was that a chance bullet might find a mark, for they were still out of effective range, and at a fast gallop they could not take careful aim. At the sound of the firing, Brady urged his men onwards and, once the last man was in the water, he kicked his horse forward forcing it into the river. Three yards from the bank the horse started swimming and Brady followed the example of the rustlers by slipping off the saddle, to take some of the weight off the animal, and, holding on to the stirrup, he was helped on by the powerful horse.

When the Bar X cowboys pulled to a halt at the edge of the river two of the men started forward again, but Bill Collins stopped them.

'Hold it,' he yelled, 'I don't want any of you risking your lives in that water. Besides, when any of them reach the other side they'll be able to pick you off easily.'

Although they were annoyed that the rustlers were escaping, the men saw the wisdom of Collins's remarks and contented themselves with firing several shots at the swimmers. They soon realised this was useless and, although some bullets hit the water near Brady, he was soon out of range.

Fighting against the pull of the fast flowing Brazo, the rustlers were strung out in a great arc as they were swept further downstream. Suddenly one man let out a piercing cry as his grip on the stirrup slackened and was finally lost. The waters took a firmer hold on him and swept him away from the animal, bundling him over and over in their onward rush until he disappeared below the surface never to appear again. A few moments later the whinny of another frightened horse sounded from the river as the struggle became too much for it and the water took a grip which would never be released. The cowboy, feeling the power go out of the horse, let go of the stirrup and struck out on his own. Slowly he fought his way on and it seemed an eternity to him before the bank drew closer. One by one the rustlers fought the torrent and reached the opposite side at various points along the bank. Men dragged themselves from the water, panting and gasping for breath, and when Brady reached safety he lay stretched out, drawing great gulps of air into his aching lungs. When he finally turned himself over he grinned at the sight of the frustrated Bar X men sitting on their horses. He pushed himself to his feet and staggered to his horse which stood a few yards away. He dragged himself into the saddle and rode slowly along the bank. Calling his men together he was relieved to find they had lost only one man and one horse.

'We were lucky to get off so lightly,' observed Mason.

'Sure,' agreed Brady. 'But we could have got away with the whole herd if we'd made sure those two Bar X men guarding the herd were dead. One of them must have got back for the Bar X outfit to get after us as quickly as they did.' He glanced round his men. 'Everyone fit to ride?'

The bedraggled, worn-out rustlers nodded and put their horses into a steady trot behind Brady.

When Bill Collins saw them move away he

shrugged his shoulders, an acceptance of the escape of the rustlers.

'Guess we may as well head back,' he said.

'What about the cattle?' asked his fore-man.

'They'll run for a while,' replied Collins, 'and no doubt they'll be well scattered, but O'Grady's outfit can pick them up in their own time. There's nothing much we can do about it.'

The cowboys bunched close together behind him as he headed in the direction of his ranch. They were about half-way there when they sighted a tell-tale dust cloud approaching and soon they recognised Dan and Clint with the drovers close behind. The two parties pulled to a halt when they met.

The ramrod looked anxiously at him. 'Did they get away?' he asked, a troubled frown creasing his brow.

'The rustlers did, but not with your cattle,' answered Collins. Some relief crossed the ramrod's face, and Bill went on to relate what had happened. 'It will take some time to round up your cattle,' he concluded, 'but at least you won't have lost many.'

'I'm mighty grateful for all you have done,' replied the ramrod, 'and I'm sorry for all the trouble that's been caused.' He turned to Dan. 'I was a fool to leave that herd just for the sake of avenging O'Grady's death. I can see now that it was all part of a plan. I guess we'll push on and try to get our cattle together.'

As the drovers rode away Dan and Clint turned their horses and rode with Bill Collins back to Bar X.

'Did you recognise any of them?' asked Dan, hoping that he might get a lead on the rustlers.

Bill Collins shook his head. 'We never got near enough,' he replied. 'Besides, they had their neckerchiefs pulled up over the lower half of their faces.'

Dan shrugged his shoulders resignedly. 'Can't be helped,' he said. 'We aren't really any nearer establishing the identity of the rustlers but Clint and I feel that they were just a little too conveniently placed when the drovers left the herd, for it to be coincidence.'

'Exactly how I felt,' agreed Bill. 'There must be some connection between the killing of Shaun O'Grady and the rustling of the herd.'

'Well I think there's something deeper than mere rustling behind all this,' said

Dan. 'In both cases the trail boss has been killed. Murdered might be a better word even though Mason killed O'Grady in self-defence.'

'I figure somethin' ought to be done about those two herds still trailing north,' put in Clint.

'Just what I was thinking,' said Dan. 'Howard is expected back some time today so we'll get a report from him then ride to meet the herds as far south as possible.'

When they reached the Bar X they were relieved to find that the doctor's report on Sloane was satisfactory and that he would recover, although care would have to be taken for some considerable time.

Dan and Clint were pleased to accept Bill Collins's invitation to stay for a meal which Charlie, the Chinese cook, soon had ready. They had finished the meal and were enjoying a cheroot whilst discussing the recent events, when the sound of an approaching horse took them outside.

'Glad to have you back, son,' called his father, as Howard dismounted in front of the house.

'It's good to be back, Pa,' answered Howard. He nodded to Dan and Clint as he stepped on to the verandah. 'All go well with you after I left, Clint?' Clint glanced at Dan and when Howard noticed the serious expression on their faces his smile disappeared. 'What's happened?' he asked.

'A whole heap of things,' said Bill Collins. 'Get washed-up and we'll tell you about it whilst you have something to eat.'

It was not long before Howard was in full possession of the recent events.

'So you see we are concerned about the two herds still trailing north; we feel that the rustlers will attack them if things go to pattern. Mason, if our suspicions are correct, will attempt to get the trail bosses.'

Howard nodded and looked thoughtful. 'I see your point,' he said. 'I found the other two herds some considerable distance behind O'Grady. My estimation is that Burt Pallister will reach the southern end of Cedar Valley tomorrow night and Seth Cunliffe is not far behind.'

'Thank goodness they won't be in the valley,' said Dan, relief showing in his voice. 'Feel like riding again tomorrow?' he asked.

Howard grinned wryly. 'I'm sure gettin' saddle sore,' he said, 'but after what you've told me nothing could stop me being right alongside you, Dan.'

Dan grinned. 'Thanks, Howard,' he said

appreciatively. 'Clint will come back to the Circle C with me tonight and we'll pick you up early in the morning.' He turned to his father-in-law. 'Do you mind keeping an eye on things in town whilst we are away?'

'Certainly not,' answered Bill Collins.

'I don't expect any trouble there,' said Dan. 'But I'll have to leave someone in charge.'

As Dan and Clint left the Bar X the sheriff's mind was full of all the possible answers to the problems which faced him, and he decided that, on their way south tomorrow, they would pay a call on Sam Brady.

7

When Dan, accompanied by Clint and Howard, had crossed the Brazo at Wayman's Ford the following morning, he informed them that he intended paying Sam Brady a visit on their way south.

'Do you think he has anything to do with the recent upheavals?' asked Howard.

'Well I've got nothing to link him with them at all,' replied Dan, 'but I'm prepared to investigate any lead to clear this business up, and the fact that Clint saw Butch Mason pay Brady a visit is enough to make me want to talk to him.'

'But he was there only a few minutes,' pointed out Clint. 'Didn't even go inside.'

'I know, but any lead is worth checking,' replied Dan.

'I think Mason is the person likely to be behind it all,' said Howard. 'He's a stranger in this area and all this trouble started after you'd seen him in Red Springs. He told you he was passing through, but he returned, so he must have been hanging around; he could have been in with the rustlers in the hills.'

'There could be something in what you say,' said Dan. 'But I feel that there is some deeper motive behind the killings and rustlings; you must admit that the tie-up between O'Grady's killing and the attempted rustling of his herd required some thought; admittedly the drovers may not have acted the way they did but someone figured they might and took the chance on them doing so by being in a position to attack the herd. I just wonder if Butch Mason really has the brains to organise anything on a big scale.'

'I doubt if he has,' agreed Clint. 'But Brady's been a hard-working, peaceable man since he came here.'

'He's a comparatively new arrival,' said Dan, 'we know little about him, he's only been operating on a small scale and may have got rather too ambitious. Matt Stevens's murder certainly wasn't linked with any rustling attempt; it appeared as if someone was deliberately out to get him.'

'Do you think Mason killed him?' asked Howard.

'Who knows?' said Dan. 'The fact that Mason got Clint off his tail seems to indicate that he was out to get O'Grady, and therefore one automatically thinks that he could have been the killer of Stevens.'

'Mason is a known hired killer,' said Howard. 'So if Brady is behind these rustlings then he could have hired Mason.'

'Could be,' replied Dan. 'So I thought we'd pay Brady a visit and see if anything crops up to give us a lead.'

The three men kept to a steady pace, conserving the energies of their horses for the long ride ahead. It was mid-morning when they topped the rise above Brady's ranch and headed for the long, low, wooden building. As they pulled to a halt outside the house Sam Brady stepped out to meet them.

'Howdy,' he greeted amiably. 'Not often I

have the pleasure of the two lawmen from Red Springs. I hope it's not trouble you're bringing.' He invited the three men inside and offered them a drink.

When Dan had taken his glass he watched Brady carefully as he put his question to him. 'There was a shooting in Red Springs yesterday; boss of one of the herds trailing north got killed by a man called Butch Mason. I wondered if, coming from Kansas, you knew him?'

Brady smiled. There was a look of amusement in his brown eyes. 'I come from Kansas, but that doesn't mean I was the associate of a hired killer that operated in that State. I knew of him, naturally, but I didn't know him.'

'Then what was he doing at this house yesterday?' Dan shot the question at Brady in a voice which was cold. If he had hoped for some startled reaction from the Kansan, Dan was disappointed, for Brady only registered surprise.

'Mason here?' he said. The question from the sheriff had surprised him, but three men, two of whom wore tin stars, had put him on his guard and he was giving nothing away. His thoughts tumbled. Someone must have seen Mason visit him. He would have to be more careful in the future. 'Oh, I see now,' he went on, as if the reason for Dan's questions had suddenly become clear. 'You mean that stranger that asked the way to Red Springs yesterday. That wasn't Butch Mason, was it?' His voice showed disbelief.

'It was,' replied Dan. There was no good beating about the bush now. 'Clint was passing here and recognised the man calling on you as Mason.'

'Well, I'll be...,' said Brady. 'Just shows, you never know to whom you are talking. As I said, he merely asked the way to Red Springs.'

'You'd never seen that man before?' queried Dan.

'I told you, he was a stranger to me,' replied Brady.

'Even though you come from Kansas?'

'Never set eyes on Mason,' answered Brady testily. 'I'll remind you Kansas is a big place.'

'Guess so,' agreed Dan. 'Thanks for your help and for the drink.' He drained his glass and handed it back to Brady. 'Guess we'd better be going.'

'Travelling far, Sheriff?' asked Brady.

'Depends on Mason,' said Dan.

'You're going to bring him in then? I thought it was self-defence.'

'Who told you that?' queried Dan.

Brady smiled to himself. The sheriff was still trying to trap him into an indiscretion. 'One of my men was in the Silver Dollar; told me about it when he got back.'

'I guess his interpretation of the shooting was correct,' replied Dan, 'but I'd like to question Mason about it.'

'Well, best of luck,' said Brady. 'Nobody was able to tag anything on him in Kansas.'

The three men took their leave and rode steadily away from the house. Once they had topped the rise and passed out of sight Dan halted the horses.

'A cool customer,' he said, 'but answer me this. Mason had been in Red Springs before riding south; why should he enquire the way on his return journey to get O'Grady?' His two companions stared at the sheriff.

'You've got a point there,' agreed Clint, a note of excitement in his voice.

'Then he must have called there for instructions,' said Howard.

'That's likely,' said Dan, 'but it was only a brief visit, so to me it would seem more likely that Mason was on to something or on some errand and merely called to inform Brady where he was going.'

'If you are right, then Brady was lying just

now about not knowing Mason,' said Clint. 'He seemed genuinely surprised.'

'He did,' agreed Dan, 'but maybe we put him on his guard. The fact that he said Mason was asking for directions puzzled me as I have said. However, probably we'll soon know. Howard, you've done a lot of riding these last few days, I'd like you to stay behind and keep an eye on Brady whilst we ride south.'

'Suits me,' said Howard.

'If anything happens and you need us we'll be with the herds, otherwise use your own discretion. I want anything that might link Brady with Mason and the rustlers. If I'm barking up the wrong tree I reckon you'll soon realise it, then I'd be grateful if you'd ride to join us.'

'Right,' said Howard and bade the two lawmen goodbye as they put their horses into a trot and headed in a southerly direction.

Howard turned his horse along the slope keeping below the skyline and made for a slight depression where an outcrop of rock rose to the edge of the hill; he secured his horse and worked his way up the rock until he had a perfect view of the ranch. There was no activity apart from two men mending fences and there was no sign of Sam Brady.

Twenty minutes passed before Howard saw the ranch-house door open and Sam Brady walk out. Howard tensed himself, watching the Kansan carefully. Brady walked briskly to the stables. Five minutes later he reappeared with a cowboy leading a horse. They exchanged a few final words before the man left the ranch at a fast gallop. Howard got the impression that there was an urgency about the whole affair and, as Brady strolled back to the house, Howard pondered on his own reaction to the scene he had witnessed. If Brady was connected with Mason and the rustlers, had he sent this man to warn them that the sheriff was nosing into things and might be getting a little too close to them? Howard wondered whether he should stay and watch Brady or trail the rider. If he was to do the latter he had only a second or two to make a decision because the man was covering the ground along the valley at a fast pace.

Suddenly Howard jumped to his feet and scrambled quickly down the rocks to his horse. He swung into the saddle, and once out of the small depression put the animal into a fast gallop on a parallel course to

Brady's cowboy, keeping below the edge of the hill until he felt far enough away from the ranch to slip over the skyline unnoticed. Howard was restless lest the rider had left the valley, but he was relieved to see the man still in sight though some considerable distance ahead. Howard put his horse down the slope and headed at a tangent into the valley. He had almost reached the bottom of the slope when he saw the rider turn off into the hills, and Howard, not wanting to lose track of the man, urged his horse faster. The powerful animal responded and, when Howard reached the shallow valley into which the man had turned, he was just in time to see him topping the right-hand slope. Howard followed and, as the terrain became steeper, the pace slowed. Throughout the rest of the morning and into the afternoon the man rode, twisting his way along one valley then another, over ridge after ridge, skirting one hill, crossing another. Howard began to wonder if the man knew he was being followed and was trying to throw him off the trail. He estimated that they must be getting fairly near the extremity of the hill country, when the man turned into a narrow valley, the sides of which were steep and rocky. After a mile along the twisting terrain, Howard saw that the sides of the valley swung round to meet in a solid wall of rock some distance ahead. He was mystified as to where the man was heading, but after a further quarter of a mile, he saw the rider making for the right-hand side of the valley at a point where the hill swung round across their path. Howard examined the hillside carefully and he saw that at that point the slope was not as steep as he had first thought. There was a narrow track which wound its way upwards across the ridge. He realised that he would have to stay and wait until the rider reached the top before he could follow; if he did not wait he would be seen. Howard curbed his impatience as he watched the man twist back and forth across the slope as he mounted higher and higher. His only fear was that by the time he had reached the top the man would have disappeared, and he would have lost all chance of locating the rustlers, for now he felt sure that the man was on his way to contact them, yet he dare not move until the rider had crossed the ridge.

As soon as the man passed out of sight, Howard kicked his horse forward and started up the narrow track with the greatest possible speed. The going was rough and stoney and the higher he went the more dangerous it became to move with any speed. Stones moved under the horse's hooves as it made its way nervously upwards. Howard encouraged it, talking softly, urging it on, but he realised it would be foolhardy to rush the animal too much, one false step and he would never get on the trail again. The slope flattened towards the ridge and Howard halted just short of the top so that by standing in the stirrups he could see over the edge. He was relieved to see the cowboy riding down a steady slope which led into a small shallow valley which was like a bowl encased by protecting hills. At the foot of the slope a fire burned forming the centre of a small encampment.

Howard's thoughts raced; he had found the rustlers' hideout! But as he watched he began to have doubts; he could not be certain; there was no proof that they were the rustlers. There was no sign of any cattle and he figured they must be hidden elsewhere. Until he saw any of these men with those cattle, he had no definite proof, nor did he know whether Butch Mason was with them. He had never seen the hired-gun, but felt certain he would be able to pick him out from Dan's description, but that would necessitate a closer look. He glanced round and seeing a slight depression in the slope on which he was standing, figured it would be a safe place to leave his horse. He stepped from the saddle and led the animal across the slope. Securing the horse, he crept up to the ridge, and studied the terrain between himself and the camp. It was well strewn with boulders, which should offer him ample cover to get close enough to the camp to study its occupants.

The cowboy whom he had been trailing had reached the camp and was surrounded by ten men with whom he was deep in conversation. Howard guessed Brady's instructions were being passed on. A few moments later the group broke up, leaving the cowboy still talking to one of the men. Howard saw the man cross to the horses when the conversation had finished. He saddled one and mounting it, crossed the valley and climbed the hill at the far side. The rest of the men were relaxing round the camp and Howard figured that this was his opportunity to get close to them.

Keeping close to the ground, so that he would be inconspicuous when he broke the skyline, he slid over the ridge and quickly sought the protection of a huge boulder. He lay behind it listening for any sign of alarm, but all was quiet and he reckoned that he had not been noticed. Howard eased himself to his feet and, in a crouching position, peered round the boulders. Seeing all was still in the camp, he slid round the rock quickly and dropped behind another boulder. Carefully picking his cover, Howard worked his way down the slope towards the camp. It was slow progress, but Howard could not afford one slip. If he was seen, or captured by these men, Dan's chances of getting to know the whereabouts of the rustlers would be as far away as ever. Howard paused for a considerable time studying the group from the cover of the boulders.

It seemed to him that men had been drifting southwards through Texas to meet in these hills; the whole thing now took on the appearance of a long planned operation. Howard searched the other men in the camp and finally found the man for whom he was looking. The man matched up with Dan's description of Butch Mason.

Howard felt he would like a closer look at the man to make absolutely certain, and if possible to overhear some of the conversation. He inched his way round the rock and started forward stealthily, his eyes watching the men below intently. They were so concerned with their own activities that he was able to get close without being observed. Now he felt sure that the man he had picked out was Mason. Howard's thoughts raced when, in one sentence, he had confirmation of all Dan's suspicions.

'I can't figure why Brady has you riding on these raids, Mason. You could do your job just as you did in Red Springs,' called a short stocky cowboy.

'You aren't paid to think,' retorted Mason harshly. 'Jest do the job you're paid to do, same as I do mine.'

Mason turned and walked to the fire where he lifted the coffee pot and poured himself a drink before sitting down beside the man whom Howard had trailed. They spoke in low voices and Howard could not hear what they were saying. From the words he had just heard he had sufficient proof that Sam Brady, Butch Mason and the rustlers were all linked and it appeared that Sam Brady was running the whole affair. Howard's only thought now was to get back to his horse and to find Dan as quickly as possible. He turned to make his way up the slope, but as he did so his left foot slipped, loosening some stones, sending them tumbling downwards. He froze in his tracks, but in his mind he knew that he would be found.

The camp had gone quiet suddenly, and as the clatter of the tumbling stones ceased, Howard could feel the tension in the air and could sense that Colts were drawn as the men stared up the slope. His hand moved to his Colt, but then he realised that it would be useless to try to fight it out, he was far out-numbered and among the rocks on the hillside it would be an easy matter for the rustlers to encircle him. He must stay alive and be able to figure out some way of getting word to Dan. If he fought he was certain to be killed, but if he allowed himself to be taken prisoner there was a chance that even these men would not shoot him in cold blood. His decision made, Howard pushed himself to his feet and immediately raised his hands above his head. As he faced the rustlers, he saw that his supposition was correct; every Colt in the camp was turned on him. For a moment no one spoke; then suddenly the silence was broken by Mason's harsh voice.

'Git down here quick if you don't want a hole drilling right through you.'

Howard stepped forward and with his

hands still raised walked into the camp. One of the men jerked Howard's Colt from its holster, and only then did Howard lower his arms. Mason stepped forward.

'Who are you and what are you doing round here?' he asked.

Before Howard could speak the man whom he had followed was beside Mason.

'I know him, Butch,' he said quickly. 'It's Howard Collins, brother-in-law of the sheriff. He was with the two lawmen when they called on Brady this morning; guess he must have stayed behind to keep an eye on the place and then followed me.'

'That was mighty careless of you,' snapped Mason.

'I checked my back trail several times,' retorted the cowboy testily, 'but it appears Collins was smarter than I was. However, there's no harm done; a bullet in the clever Mister Collins and we are back where we started from.'

'Not exactly,' rapped Mason. 'If he was with the lawmen then McCoy will be suspicious when he doesn't show up. For some reason he must have suspected Brady – why he should do so puzzles me, otherwise he wouldn't have left Collins behind. A bullet doesn't answer our problem. We'll have to wait for instructions from Brady.'

One of the rustlers stepped forward. 'There's only one answer to a nosey parker,' he hissed. 'Are you afraid to use that gun, Mason?' There was a note of mockery in the man's voice.

Mason's eyes narrowed, smouldering angrily. His fist flashed upwards taking the man full between the eyes before he realised it. The cowboy crashed backwards on the hard ground. His hand clawed at his gun but before he touched it, Mason's gun was in his hand menacing the man on the ground.

'Don't try that again,' snapped Mason angrily, 'or maybe you'll find out whether I can use a gun or not. We'll let Brady decide about Collins.' His words were emphatic and no one else questioned them. 'Right, tie Collins up.'

Two men grabbed Howard by the arms and in a few minutes he was securely tied and then dumped unceremoniously behind a rock. He tested his bonds but found it was useless to try to loosen them; the two men had seen to it that there was no hope of that. Howard cursed himself for being so careless. He had enough information for Dan to arrest Sam Brady but now there seemed little hope of Dan being able to use it; he suffered no illusions as to what his eventual fate would be, but he took some comfort from the fact that he was still alive. Although he could see only one end to his predicament, there was still some chance that something might turn up in his favour.

8

Dan McCoy and Clint Schofield put their horses into a long, steady lope after leaving Howard. They wanted to reach Burt Pallister's herd before it reached Cedar Valley, and, if Howard's assumption that it would be at the south end of the valley that night was correct, they had to keep at a quick pace to reach it by nightfall. Throughout the day their eyes constantly searched the hills bordering the valley but they saw no sign of anyone. It was with some relief that they reached the end of Cedar Valley and saw the herd some distance across the grassland.

'Guess Pallister's been held up,' said Dan. 'He appears to be bedding the herd down.'

'That means it will be safe from attack,' observed Clint. 'I reckon there's too much open country between the hills and the herd for the rustlers to hit it tonight or first thing in the morning.'

'That's true,' agreed Dan. 'But it also means that Pallister won't clear Cedar Valley tomorrow, and a night in the valley will give the rustlers the same opportunity as they had against O'Grady's herd.'

Clint rubbed his stubbled chin thoughtfully. 'I guess there's not much we can do about that except be well prepared for the attack.'

'After what we have to tell Pallister I reckon he'll be more ready to listen to advice than O'Grady was,' said Dan. 'If he'll camp in the same place, the rustlers can use the same tactics, and you, having some pre-knowledge of that, can advise Pallister how to position his men.'

Clint agreed but looked thoughtful as they rode on. Burt Pallister gave them a warm welcome when they reached the herd and, leaving the bedding down to his ramrod, rode with them to the chuck-wagon.

'I'm mighty pleased to see you,' said Pallister. 'Howard told me about rustlers; have you got them cleared out yet?'

'Not yet,' said Dan. 'It's been hard to get a lead on them but we're exploring one or two possibilities. The most important thing is to get your herd through without losing any of them to the rustlers. I'd hoped you would be nearer Cedar Valley so as you could travel through it in one day.'

'So had I,' said Pallister, 'but we haven't had the best of luck on this drive and more than one thing went wrong today and held us back. I'm just going to have to take the risk of spending tomorrow night in the valley.'

'Clint and I have been talking that over, and we figure that if you stop in the same place as O'Grady did, the rustlers will try the same tactics and you could have a nice little surprise waiting for them.'

Pallister agreed, and, whilst the three men enjoyed a meal, Clint outlined the plan of the raid on O'Grady's herd and advised Pallister about positioning his men. Drovers, weary from the day's work, rode in, handed over their horses to the young Mexican in charge of the remuda, and, in spite of their remarks, eagerly accepted the food prepared by the cook. Clint watched them thoughtfully, wondering which of them might be killed when the rustlers attacked the herd. They accepted that possibility when they signed up to drive a herd north, but Clint began to feel that if the raid could be prevented so much the better.

The light was beginning to fade from the sky when he drew Dan to one side.

'I've been doing some thinking,' he said. 'These rustlers must be keeping a check on these herds; an' I figure that it is likely that they'll have a look-out on that promontory at the end of Cedar Valley. I reckon if we could get a lead on him, we might get on to the rustlers.'

Dan smiled. 'All right, Clint; I know you like to play a lone hand at times and I agree with you; a man up there could lead you to the rustlers' hide-out.'

'Wal, I know those hills, Dan,' said Clint, 'an' you can be sure that if there's a man up there I'll find him. He's got to keep watch until the morning, now that the herd's out here; I figure he'll wait until the herd's moving before he reports back to his camp.'

'Right,' agreed Dan, 'but don't go until it's dark; then you'll probably get into the hill country without being seen. If I'm not here with the herd when you return take what action you think necessary and we'll ask Pallister to place his drovers at your disposal if you want them.'

'I thought you were going to stay with the herd,' commented Clint curiously.

'You aren't the only one who's been doing some thinking,' smiled Dan. 'The thing which has stuck in my mind about this whole affair is the killing of Matt Stevens and Shaun O'Grady; both were trail bosses and I think the killings were made to fit in with rustling activities.'

'You think Mason has some connection with the rustlers?' queried Clint.

'I feel that he would,' replied Dan, 'and as the raid on O'Grady's herd in Sundance Hollow seemed to be linked with his killing, it would seem that Mason is in on the whole affair. Through Mason there may be a link with Brady. It seems to me as if someone has got it in for trail bosses. I'm going to send for Seth Cunliffe and take him, along with Burt Pallister, to have a look at Brady.'

'Maybe he has a link with their past,' said Clint.

\Dan nodded. 'Exactly. We know these four men have always driven cattle north at the same time and they have always passed through Kansas. Brady comes from Kansas.'

Clint looked thoughtful. 'You may be on the right track there, Dan. If there was ever any trouble in Kansas then Seth and Burt should recognise Brady.'

'It's a long shot,' pointed out Dan, 'but I

reckon it's worth trying.'

'Wal, best of luck, Dan,' said Clint.

'Same goes for you, too,' said Dan with a grin. 'With a bit of luck now we shall soon see an end to this affair, but it looks as if Howard has nothing to report.'

Dan watched Clint ride away into the darkness thankful that he had a loyal and experienced deputy. He turned and strolled thoughtfully to Burt Pallister.

'Burt,' said Dan, 'I'm going to ask you to leave the herd tomorrow and ride with me to look someone over.'

The trail boss looked surprised and there was concern on his face when he protested. 'I can't leave the herd when it's heading into Cedar Valley and is likely to be attacked by rustlers.'

'That's one reason why I want you to leave,' said Dan. 'I've told you what has been going on over these last few days; two trail bosses have been killed and I have a feeling you'll be next on the list.'

'What!' Burt cried. 'Aren't you reading more into these things than there is?'

'I might be,' replied Dan, 'but I want to take precautions. There's a hired killer riding these hills, he killed O'Grady and I reckon it was he who killed Stevens; he's no cattleman and I figure he's here to get his own revenge or hired by someone else.'

Pallister looked thoughtful. 'I appreciate your concern but I can look after myself; I must stay with the herd.'

'That's exactly what Stevens and O'Grady would have said,' countered Dan, 'and I realise that your first duty is to get those cattle through, but both Stevens and O'Grady are buried down by the Brazo. You'll be helping yourself if you come with me.'

'I don't like it,' said Pallister doubtfully.

'Look at it this way,' went on Dan, 'when the rustlers attack, Mason could be with them to get at you during the upheaval. I reckon he tried to get both Stevens and O'Grady that way, failed, then tagged the herd until he got the opportunity. That happened in the case of Stevens when there was trouble at the Brazo, but when O'Grady got safely across something had to be done.'

'If Mason is out for revenge then you can rule me as safe,' replied Pallister. 'I've never tangled with him. Stevens and O'Grady might have done, but I've never heard them talk about it.'

'Supposing someone had hired him,' pressed Dan.

'Who?' smiled Burt as if he was dubious of

Dan's theory.

'Does the name Sam Brady mean anything to you?' asked the sheriff.

'Brady?' Pallister muttered the word half to himself as if trying to recall some association with it. He shook his head slowly. 'Sorry, Dan, the name means nothing to me.'

'Then ride with me tomorrow,' urged Dan, 'and look this Sam Brady over.'

'Look here, Dan, I want to be with my herd when it moves into Cedar Valley tomorrow an' I must be around when we expect the rustlers to strike.'

'That's one time you aren't going to be around,' replied Dan sharply. 'I think your life's in danger and I'm going to see you safely out of the way, even if it means taking you at the point of a gun.'

The trail boss stiffened. His face, lit by the flickering flames of the campfire, clouded with anger. Words of protestation sprung to his lips but were halted by Dan.

'I'll compromise with you,' Dan went on quickly. 'We'll ride with the herd until it's bedded down. You've got a good crew and a first-class ramrod; if you brief them thoroughly they can take care of things. We'll ride after camp has been made and be in position to see Brady the following morning.'

Pallister could tell from the determined tone in Dan's voice that he would not be put off. He knew Dan well, respected his position, and concern. He did not want to be difficult over this affair and he figured that if the sheriff was prepared to meet him he should do the same.

'Very well,' he replied. 'I don't like leaving the herd, but if your theory is right it might work out for the best in the long run.'

'Thanks, Burt,' said Dan sincerely. 'There's one more request I'd like to make.'

Burt laughed. 'You never give up, do you, Dan? Wal, what is it? I'll try to oblige.'

'You said Seth Cunliffe was pressing you close. Wal, I'd like you to ride with me to see him.'

'If that's all then I'm as good as in the saddle,' said Burt. He pushed himself to his feet, stretched himself and picked up his Stetson. 'I'm ready to hit the blankets; will we be very long?'

'No, I don't think so,' answered Dan. 'How far away is he?'

'About three miles,' replied Burt.

The two men were soon in the saddles and left the camp at a brisk trot. They swung wide of Seth Cunliffe's herd so they would not disturb the steers and made for the fire marking the position of the drovers' camp.

'Hello!' shouted Burt when they saw firelit figures move at the sound of their approach. 'It's Burt Pallister and Dan McCoy!'

'Howdy,' yelled back a deep gruff voice. They saw a burly figure step forward to meet them and as they swung from the saddles Seth Cunliffe greeted them. 'What brings you here, Dan?' Seth shook hands with the two men firmly. His greeting was amiable but filled with curiosity. He felt that a visit from the sheriff spelt trouble somewhere.

'There's been trouble up ahead,' replied Dan, 'and I've come to ask you to co-operate in a scheme which, I hope, will help to clear it up.'

'Let's hear about it over a cup of coffee,' replied Seth.

Burt and Dan sat down and when Seth handed them some coffee Dan related the happenings of the past few days.

'I'm sure sorry about Stevens and O'Grady,' said Seth, 'but I don't know any reason why Butch Mason should go gunning for me.'

'Do you know anyone by the name of Sam Brady?' asked Dan, having kept Brady's name out of the story up to this point.

'I'm afraid the name means nothing to

me,' replied Seth. 'Who is he?'

'I have an idea he might be behind the whole affair,' replied Dan, 'but I can't prove it. Burt has agreed to look him over and I'd like you to be along to see if you can recognise him.'

'Sure I'll come,' agreed Seth.

'Good,' said Dan making no attempt to hide his pleasure that Seth had agreed so readily. Dan went on to outline his plan regarding Pallister's herd. 'Burt and I are going to move off when the herd is bedded down. I think the rustlers will make an attack when his herd is in the valley. I would like you to hold your herd here tomorrow so that the rustlers will not be tempted to attack you instead.'

'Right,' agreed Seth. 'The boys will welcome a break; we've been pushing hard. I'll join you some time tomorrow.'

'Thanks,' said Dan. 'I'm mighty grateful to both of you for your co-operation.'

When Dan and Burt had returned to their camp, sleep did not come easily to the sheriff. His mind was occupied with the plans he had made and their possible outcome.

9

As he rode away from the camp Clint Schofield knew he was playing a long shot, but
anything was better than waiting. Knowing
the hill country as he did he felt sure that, if
the rustlers had a look-out above the end of
Cedar Valley, he could find him.

The Texas night was starlit and Clint kept
to a brisk trot wanting to reach the hills
before the moon rose to flood the countryside with revealing light. After passing the
herd, around which he heard the out of
tune, but soothing lilt of the night-riders, he
swung across the grassland making for the
hills on the eastern side of Cedar Valley.

If the supposed look-out spotted the
shadowy figure of a lone rider Clint wanted
to create the impression that he was heading
for the hills on the opposite side of the valley
to those in which the rustlers had their hide-
out. Reaching the hills, Clint kept close to
them until he felt satisfied that, if his
presence were known, he would have been
taken for a man bent on some destination

beyond the valley. He turned his horse and rode quickly across the valley and sought out an old track which wound its way upwards to the top of the hills.

The side of the hill was in a deep shadow and Clint had to exercise the utmost care in negotiating the rough, narrow track. He had a strong reliable horse and the deputy sheriff encouraged it with softly spoken words. For all his experience of these old tracks, Clint was somewhat relieved when he reached the top of the hills and moved out on to a broad ridge.

Clint kept his horse to a walking pace as he moved towards the promontory at the corner of the hills, at the same time he edged to his right towards a hollow which ran parallel with the ridge. He worked his way along carefully; a slight noise would attract the attention of any watcher in the hills. About a mile further on the hollow began to rise steadily to form a ridge at the edge of the hills and Clint pulled to a halt at the bottom of the rise. He was directly below the promontory forming the corner of the hills. He slipped from the saddle and led his horse to a small cutting into the ridge, and, in the black shadow secured his horse. Clint gave it a friendly reassuring pat before moving stealthily away to start the climb back on the ridge. He traversed the rise quickly and, as he moved on to the ridge, he dropped to his stomach and crept behind a boulder. From this position he surveyed the hundred yards to the promontory. The moon which had risen during his ride, now lit the hills with a pale silvery light. Clint saw that he had about fifty yards of open ground to negotiate before he reached the upheaval of rocks which crowned the promontory at the corner of the hills.

This was an ideal place for a man to keep watch; he was above Cedar Valley and had a wide view of the plains beyond. From here he could easily keep close check on any herd moving into the valley. If Clint's surmise was correct, this was the place he must surely find the man whom he expected was keeping a watch on the herds. He could be anywhere in that upheaval of rocks, and Clint realised his task of finding the man without being detected would be difficult. He could wait where he was until daylight and trail the man when he moved; he figured the look-out would be a stranger to the area and would not chance moving through the hills in the darkness, besides he would have nothing to report until Burt Pallister's herd moved the next morning. But if there was no look-out Clint would have wasted all the night. He had to make certain that somebody else was there.

Keeping to the ground Clint crept forward, Indian fashion, covering the open fifty yards as quickly as possible hoping that the man's direction was attracted out across the plain. Reaching the first boulders he paused, listening intently, but no sound reached his ears. If there was anyone close by Clint felt sure he had not been detected. He peered cautiously round the boulder surveying the ground ahead. The moonlight played tricks among the rocks casting deep shadows, working a quilt of light and dark so that rocks loomed large, taking on shapes which made the imagination run wild. Twice Clint thought that he saw the shape of a man, but then realised it wasn't. He inched forward, picking his way carefully, making sure his foot did not scrape a rock. Suddenly he froze, a blackness loomed in the shape of a horse, but as his eyes penetrated the dark patch, he realised the shape was too still; besides it would have been difficult to get a horse into that position, and Clint knew that, like he had done, the man would have left his horse at a convenient place a short distance away.

Clint moved forward carefully between the rocks. If his supposition regarding a look-out was correct, Clint knew he must come across him soon for he was nearing the cliff-like corner of the hills.

He had moved five more yards when suddenly he stopped, hardly daring to breathe, excitement seizing him. A few yards ahead and slightly above him there was a small faint glow in the deep shadow of a huge boulder. Clint strained his eyes trying to pierce the blackness, but he could not make out any form; only the glow brightened momentarily then faded again, moved in a small arc, then back again to brighten, then fade again. Clint thanked his luck that he had reached this position whilst the man was smoking a cigarette. Had he not done so he would never have seen the man and would have been seen himself. Clint waited a few minutes then moved carefully backwards until he reached the cover of a boulder where he relaxed whilst he made up his mind what to do.

With a decision made he worked his way noiselessly to the edge of the rocks then speedily across the open ground to the first boulder he had used as cover at the top of the slope out of the hollow. Whilst this would be an advantageous position to observe the man when he left, Clint wanted to be able to see the herd as well. He looked round and noticed a shadow close to the edge of the hill overlooking the valley. Knowing this must indicate a depression in the ground, Clint crossed quickly to it and found himself in a hollow sufficiently deep enough to keep him out of sight and yet afford him a view into the valley and beyond to the plains. Satisfied with his position, Clint settled down for the night eagerly awaiting the next dawn which, he felt, would bring with it a chance of finding the rustlers.

When the first light flooded into the tiny hollow, Clint woke out of his shallow sleep. He had dozed and woken continuously throughout the night, but now, with the coming of daylight, he was awake and alert. An hour later he saw the herd begin to move slowly towards Cedar Valley, and, for most of the next two hours, Clint kept his attention concentrated on the rocks with only an occasional glance at the herd. Clint was beginning to think that the man was not going to make a move when suddenly he appeared and hurried across the intervening space to a smaller group of rocks. Clint tensed himself, ready for instant action as soon as the intentions of the man were clear. A few moments later he reappeared with a horse, swung into the saddle and headed into the hills.

The deputy sheriff did not lose any time in following the rider. At all costs he must keep close to him; he could not afford to lose him now. Clint scrambled quickly down the slope into the hollow, untied his horse, swung into the saddle, and put the animal into a gallop, guiding it in the direction taken by the man. He checked the horse's pace as he neared the top of a rise and was relieved to see the rustler at the bottom of a long slope leading into a valley. For half an hour Clint skilfully followed the man, keeping him in sight without being seen. Whenever the rider topped a rise Clint quickened his pace so that he could be certain which direction the man had taken on the other side. It was on one such occasion when Clint reached the top of a rise that he tugged his horse to a stop and almost immediately turned it sharply below the skyline. His sight of the other side of the rise had been brief but it had been sufficient for him to realise that he had reached the rustlers' hideout.

He slipped from the saddle and crept

quickly to the top of the rise. Removing his Stetson he peered cautiously over the ridge and saw the rustlers' camp situated at one side of the huge saucer-shaped hollow. When he saw the rustlers climb to their feet he realised that they had seen the rider. He scrambled away from the top of the rise, rose to his feet and hurried to his horse. Clint's first inclination was to ride for Dan, but he realised that with the arrival of the look-out plans would be made and he felt it important that he should overhear those plans and thereby be able to anticipate their actions.

To get near to the camp he must ride round the rim of the hollow. Knowing he had no time to waste he pushed the horse into a gallop, keeping well below the skyline. When he estimated that he was within earshot of the camp he slowed his horse to a walking pace so that he would not be heard. Impatient as he was to reach an advantageous position quickly he realised that discovery would spoil every chance of success. Judging he was as far as he dare go on horseback, Clint slipped from the saddle, secured his horse and moved swiftly up the slope until he could see into the hollow.

The camp was only a short distance to his right, and he saw the rustlers eager for news crowding round the man whom he had followed. Clint slipped over the edge of the hollow and using every available cover made his way down the slope until he was within earshot of the camp.

'Well, what's the plan now?' called one of the men.

'You're certain that herd won't get through Cedar Valley in daylight,' said Mason addressing the man who had just ridden in.

'Yes,' came the reply. 'I reckon they'll bed down the herd tonight in the same place as O'Grady did.'

Mason rubbed his chin thoughtfully. 'Wal, that's convenient of them,' he smiled.

'Same tactics as we employed there last time?' asked one of the rustlers.

'With those two lawmen about we'd better be careful,' continued another.

Clint stiffened at this remark. How did the rustlers know that he and Dan were in the hill country? Did this signify that Brady was in with them and had sent them word after they had called upon him?

'Did you see anything of them?' asked Mason of the man who had been the lookout.

'Two hombres were riding in the direction of the herd when I reached the promontory, but I couldn't see who they were.'

'Wal, let's suppose it was them,' said Mason. 'They would warn the trail boss about what's been happening. Knowing how we hit O'Grady's herd they will expect us to hit this one in the same way and at the same time and might even be bedding down the herd in the same place hoping we'll do just that. Wal, we'll give them a big surprise. There'll be plenty of moon tonight so we'll hit the herd about midnight.'

'That'll sure surprise them,' shouted someone, and the rest of the rustlers laughed when they thought of the surprise the weary drovers would receive.

'Right, we'll leave here well before dark so that we can be in position to see the herd bed down for the night. We'll make our final plans then. I reckon if they are expecting an attack at dawn there won't be extra guards at midnight.'

Clint stiffened when he realised the shock which would await the drovers unless he could warn them in time. He was about to move off to his horse when he froze, shocked to his very heart by the next remark.

'Someone will have to guard Collins whilst we're away tonight; it had better be you seeing that you were up nearly all last night.'

Mason indicated the look-out man.

Collins! Clint's thoughts raced; it must be Howard. He looked round but could see him nowhere, but he could well be hidden behind one of several boulders or even directly below him, a position he could not see from his hiding place. Howard must have followed someone from Brady's ranch only to get caught, Clint's thoughts pounded. The herd would be at the mercy of the rustlers unless he warned the drovers, and yet he could not leave Howard here. If he waited until there was only one man left guarding Howard he could, in all probability, rescue him, but then he might be too late to warn the drovers. Clint was torn between two decisions, but finally `decided that he could not leave Howard; his life could easily be in danger especially if the rustlers returned angry at the failure of their raid.

Clint settled down keeping the camp under close observation and studying its layout. Howard's position became known when the rustlers were having a meal and one of them took a plate of stew to someone out of Clint's view almost immediately below his hiding place.

During the afternoon Clint sensed that the rustlers were impatient to be getting on the move and he was pleased when they decided to move out earlier than he had anticipated. Excitement rose in him as he watched the activity in the camp.

'Are you riding with us, Mason?' called out one of the men.

'Sure,' replied the hired gunman. 'I hope to get Burt Pallister during this raid.'

Attention gripped Clint. It was imperative to reach the herd in time in case Dan had altered his plans and not taken Burt with him to identify Brady. Clint watched the rustlers leave and waited impatiently willing time to pass until the rustlers were out of gunshot hearing.

When he decided it was time to make his move Clint drew his Colt from his holster and started down the slope. The guard, who had been sitting on the grass smoking a cigarette, suddenly pushed himself to his feet, threw the remains of his cigarette away and walked to the fire where he reached for a jug of coffee.

Clint, surprised by the man's sudden movement, froze in his tracks, but as the man reached the fire he started forward again still crouching low using the rocks as cover. Suddenly his right foot slipped on a sharp rock sending a shower of stones rolling down the remaining few yards to the hollow. Clint cursed to himself as he almost lost his balance which threw him from the cover. Startled by the noise the rustler spun round and a sharp gasp of surprise broke from his lips when he saw Clint. His right hand clawed for his gun, but Clint, who had been quick to restore his balance, squeezed the trigger of his Colt before the gun cleared the leather. The bullet drummed into the man's stomach; a look of surprised horror crossed the rustler's face as his left hand grasped at the pain. His knees started to buckle, the Colt had come out of its holster and even as he pitched forward his finger tightened on the trigger. There was a roar and the bullet splintered a rock a few yards in front of him. Clint stepped cautiously forward keeping the silent form covered with his gun.

'Clint!' A gasp of surprise broke from Howard's lips when he reached the bottom of the slope.

Clint's eyes did not leave the rustler. 'Howdy, Howard, you all right?' he asked.

'Sure, jest get me out of these ropes as quickly as possible.'

'Be with you in a minute,' said Clint and hurried forward to the still form. A quick glance told him the man was dead; he turned on his heels and ran to Howard, holstering his gun as he did so. He pulled out a knife and two quick strokes released Howard from his bonds.

'Am I mighty glad to see you,' smiled Howard, slapping his old friend on the shoulder. 'We're going to have to move fast,' he went on. 'This outfit is going to attack Pallister's herd at midnight.'

'I know,' replied Clint. 'I followed that hombre from his look-out. I've been up amongst the rocks ever since and I over-heard their plans.' He related quickly what had happened after he and Dan had left Howard watching Brady's ranch.

'I sure hope Dan has got Burt Pallister to look Brady over,' said Howard. 'That will keep him out of Mason's way – it sure seems that Dan's theories were right; shortly after you left me, Brady sent a man into the hills, I followed him but unfortunately I was careless and got caught.'

'Lucky they didn't kill you there and then,' said Clint.

'Some of them wanted to, but Mason told them it should be left to Brady.'

'Are you ready to ride?' asked Clint.

Howard nodded and hurried to find his horse. Leading it, he followed Clint until they

151

reached the deputy's mount. Darkness was gathering over the hill country south of the Brazo and the two riders put their horses into a gallop in the direction of Cedar Valley.

10

Once Burt Pallister had his herd moving, Dan felt easier. The waiting of the previous night had not been helped by the fact that Dan knew that somewhere in the darkened Texas countryside, Clint and Howard were each playing a lone hand in an attempt to bring the rustlers, and the man behind them, to justice. Once daylight had come and he was on the move some of the tension went out of Dan. Twenty-four hours from now he reckoned he would know whether his theory was correct or not. Whilst Dan felt sure that Butch Mason was linked with the rustlers and would not make an attempt on Pallister's life in daylight, he kept a close watch on the trail boss.

He admired the way in which Pallister handled his crew so that the cattle were not pressed too hard, but kept fairly compact to avoid too much straggling.

When they entered Cedar Valley, Dan rode closer to Pallister and kept a close watch on the hillside, but saw nothing to arouse his suspicions. It was late afternoon when they reached the point where they had agreed to bed down the herd, and, once the herd was settled, the drovers fell eagerly into the meal which had been prepared by the cook. Whilst they were eating, Seth Cunliffe rode in. Dan was pleased he had arrived in good time because he sensed, from the remarks he had been making, that Burt was wishing that he had not promised to leave the herd.

'We will leave just as it's getting dark,' said Dan, after he and Pallister had greeted Cunliffe.

'It's against my grain to leave my herd,' remarked Pallister.

'I know how you feel,' said Dan. 'But believe me, if it wasn't important, I wouldn't ask you to do it.'

Pallister briefed his ramrod and drovers about the possibility of a raid by the rustlers, and, by the time they had made their plans, the light was fading in Cedar Valley.

'I reckon you'd all better git some sleep as soon as possible,' concluded Burt, 'and be in your positions about an hour before dawn.'

Detecting the concern and reluctance to leave them in his voice, the ramrod hastened to assure him that all would be well.

Half an hour later, Dan, together with the two trail bosses, was heading along the darkened valley. Once the moon came up Dan quickened his pace and, when they were clear of the valley, swung into a wide arc until they were riding along a low ridge. As the hill steepened, Dan kept below the ridge top and, after travelling for two miles, he pulled to a halt; Burt and Seth stopped beside him.

'Brady's place is in the valley on the other side of this ridge. I reckon we will be opposite his house about another mile further on.'

The two men nodded. 'What's your plan?' asked Pallister.

'I reckon on moving as close as possible to the house, then lying up there until daylight,' said Dan, 'then we can keep the place under observation until you see Brady.'

'No way of tackling him tonight?' asked Burt. 'I'm anxious to git back to the herd.'

'I appreciate that,' replied Dan, 'but I want you to see Brady without being seen. If we try to get too close tonight, someone may see us and then things will start to go wrong.'

Dan kicked his horse forward and the two

cattlemen followed him. After a further mile Dan halted beside a group of rocks, told the two men to stay where they were, slipped from his saddle and hurried to the top of the ridge. A few moments later he was back with Burt and Seth.

'We're almost opposite the ranch-house,' he said. 'We'll leave the horses here.' The two men slipped from their saddles and after they had secured their horses amongst the rocks, Dan led them to the top of the ridge. They dropped below the skyline and stopped to survey the moonlit valley. At the bottom of the slope and a short distance to their right lay the long, low, wooden building.

'I reckon if we go to that clump of shrubs we should be in a good position to see Brady when he comes out in the morning,' said Dan. 'There appears to be a gulley running back up this slope from those bushes, and that should afford us ample cover when we want to leave tomorrow.'

Seth and Burt agreed with the sheriff and the three men crept down the slope to the shrubs indicated by Dan. There they found they were afforded ample cover from which to view the house, and they settled down to await daylight.

The rustlers kept to a steady pace through the hills and reached their position above the herd whilst there was some measure of daylight left.

'They're sure set up right for us,' grinned Mason as he surveyed the herd which had just been bedded down for the night. He glanced round. 'A clear sky and bright moon; we should have no difficulty in taking them,' he added.

'Same plan as before?' asked one of the men.

He looked thoughtful whilst he studied the herd. 'No,' he replied. 'I reckon we can forget the remuda. If we hit the herd from the north we can drive them straight down the valley and swing them north into the hills. We'll forget any strays and keep the main bunch moving.' He detailed four men to take up positions above the camp and keep the drovers pinned down by rifle fire. 'That takes care of our set-up until near midnight.' Mason settled down and studied the camp through his spy-glass and noted that Sheriff McCoy was amongst the men below.

'Hombre riding in from the south,' reported one of the rustlers.

Mason swung his spy-glass on to the lone rider and drew him into focus. 'Wal, I'm goin' to git all the birds in one shoot,' he muttered to himself. 'This hombre answers Brady's description of Seth Cunliffe. Now I'll have three to take and the job will be finished.' Whilst he was pleased at the prospect of an early end to his job Mason wondered why Cunliffe was riding into Pallister's camp.

'Are you riding with us?' queried one of the men.

'So far,' answered Mason, 'then during the disturbance I hope to get close to the camp whilst our four men on the hillside keep the cowpokes pinned down.'

The rustlers relaxed on the hill above the herd unaware that, as darkness covered the countryside, three men rode out of the drovers' camp.

Clint and Howard kept their horses to a brisk pace. At first the going was rough and of necessity their pace was not as fast as they would have liked. Clint led the way across two rough ridges before turning into a long narrow valley. He quickened the pace as much as he dare. The climb out of the valley was steep and the horses had to be coaxed with encouraging words. Earth loosened under the animals' hooves and stones tumbled behind them down the slope.

Some measure of relief came to the two men once they had gained the top of the difficult climb. When they reached the top they found the going easier. The valleys were shallower and the hills rounder, and when they came on to a broad hillside, in the gathering darkness, Howard drew alongside Clint.

'Think we'll make it?' he called.

The grizzle-faced deputy nodded. There was a grim determination in his eyes. 'We should,' he replied, 'provided there is no mishap. When we get to the edge of the hills overlooking Cedar Valley we'll have to watch out for the rustlers. I'm calculating that they'll be above the herd ready to use a gulley which runs at a gentle angle down the hillside and will bring them into the valley on the north side of the herd. I know a path further north which we will use. It will be a bit tricky, especially as there will be no moonlight on that part of the hill, but at the same time it will make it less likely that the rustlers will spot us.'

A few miles further on Clint led the way into a shallow hollow which rose gently to the edge of the hills. He slowed the pace, and although Howard was anxious to reach the herd, he did not question the action of the older man. Shortly before reaching the end of the hollow Clint pulled to a halt.

'This hollow runs out on to the edge of the hills overlooking Cedar Valley; immediately opposite to it is the path which we must take. For a brief moment we'll be on the skyline. Keep close to me and move quickly. We'll have to take the chance of being seen by the rustlers, but we'll be unfortunate if we are, because I reckon their attention won't be directed this way. When we reach Cedar Valley we'll keep close to the hillside because it will be in the shadow.'

'Right, Clint,' replied Howard.

The deputy sheriff sent his horse forward at a walking pace up the slope. He paused just below the top; checked that Howard was close behind him, then stabbed his horse forward urging it over the rise and on to the path. Howard followed Clint's action but was a little too quickly on to the path and taken unawares by its narrowness in spite of Clint's previous warning. His horse stumbled, and only superb handling by Howard and a ready answer from the horse prevented the animal sliding off the path down the hillside.

Clint heard the horse stumble but dare not stop now that he was on the path but, hearing no noise of bodies crashing down the hillside, he realised that all was well. Howard whispered to his horse, soothing the fright out of it. It was not easy to see the path and so Howard was particular to keep close to the black figure in front of him. Steadily the two men descended the twisting path. Clint knew it was essential to reach the drovers' camp as quickly as possible, but he also knew that undue haste could be their undoing; one false step could prove fatal.

It seemed an age before the path began to flatten out and then, almost before they realised it, they were in the valley. They relaxed in their saddles, and when Howard was about to send his horse quickly forward, Clint whispered.

'Steady, son. We must not rouse the camp or the rustlers will get the impression that something is wrong. We want to have a surprise reception for that gang.'

Howard realised the wisdom of Clint's words and, when Clint put his horse into a walking pace, he matched it. Some distance ahead they could see the glow of the camp-fire, and when they neared it, they could see the sleeping forms of the drovers. Only one man was awake and he was seated on the edge of the light cast by the fire. They were close to the camp before the man heard the faint clop of their hooves and they saw him turn in their direction, easing his rifle upwards so that it was ready for instant action. He moved slowly sideways from the firelight but by the glow of the moon they saw him stop beside a blanketed form on the ground. The blankets moved and a man rose to his feet. Clint pulled his horse to a halt.

'Deputy Sheriff Clint Schofield,' he called out softly in order to identify himself.

They could sense the two drovers relax and heard one of them call out quietly.

'Come right in.'

Clint and Howard tapped their horses forward and a few moments later halted beside the chuck-wagon. They swung from the saddle and were joined by the guard and the ramrod of the outfit.

'Glad to see you back, Clint,' greeted the ramrod. 'Any luck?'

'Sure,' replied Clint. 'Just as well I did go. The rustlers had captured Howard Collins, but I managed to rescue him after the rustlers had left their camp. They are somewhere on the hills planning to attack you at midnight.'

'What!' gasped the ramrod. 'That isn't what we anticipated.'

'Certainly isn't,' said Clint. 'It's a good job I was able to tag on to them.'

'I'll rouse everyone; we've very little more than half an hour,' said the ramrod.

'Hold it,' said Clint. 'Don't rush things.'

'Be we...,' started the ramrod, mystified by Clint's casualness.

'I know we must move fast,' replied Clint, 'but, if the rustlers are watching this camp, excessive activity would arouse their suspicions. Warn your men individually, tell them to get up discreetly, leave their blankets to make it appear they're still under them and get around to the other side of this wagon without too much disturbance.'

'Tell them to keep away from the firelight,' added Howard.

The ramrod and the guard crept quietly away and moved around the camp, waking each man in turn, whispering Clint's instructions. One by one the drovers slid out of their blankets and, leaving them in position, crawled away to the chuck-wagon where Clint and Howard were waiting for them. When they had all assembled, Clint issued his instructions quickly, and one by one the drovers slid away to the shadows on the hillside. They made their way to the bottom of the gulley which Clint reckoned the rustlers would use to reach the valley. Once there, they ranged themselves along the hillside overlooking the gulley.

Clint was tense as they waited. He hoped his supposition would be correct; if the rustlers had already descended to the valley and were hidden in the shadows then his efforts would be in vain. The minutes, charged with tension, went by too slowly. Howard, beside him, grew restless.

'It must be after midnight,' he whispered. 'Maybe they've changed their plans.'

'Could be,' replied Clint, 'but we must wait here. They won't be fixed to half an hour or so.'

'I could scout up the hillside,' suggested Howard.

The older man shook his head. 'No, if you are seen it would betray our presence.'

An uneasy silence, broken only by the distant sound of the cattle in the valley, spread over the men on the hillside. Suddenly Clint stiffened. He grasped Howard's arm, and Collins saw the deputy incline his head, listening intently. There was a faint scuffle high up on the hillside. It faded and then was repeated. Gradually it grew louder, became identifiable as horses' hooves descending the gulley at a walking pace. As the sound grew nearer, shadowy forms became discernible, and Clint eased his rifle upwards.

When he judged that the rustlers were opposite the drovers he raised his rifle to his shoulder and squeezed the trigger. The crash reverberated across the hillside and was the signal for pandemonium. The drovers fired quickly into the gulley at any shadowy form they thought was a man. The rustlers, taken completely by surprise, dived for cover and rapidly returned the fire. Flashes split the darkness and bullets whined between drovers and rustlers. Horses, released from their riders' grip, panicked and raced down the gulley to gallop across the valley away from the shattering noise.

When he saw the animals start to gallop down the hillside Howard drew a line on a man still seated in his saddle, but, before he could squeeze the trigger, he saw the man slide sideways and, realising the man was using the horse's body as a protection against the bullets, Howard turned his gun away.

'One of them escaping,' he yelled to Clint.

'One doesn't matter,' shouted Clint. 'He can't rustle a herd on his own.'

Howard grinned. Now that the action had started he felt some of the tension of the last few hours go out of him. Suddenly there was a crack of gunfire behind them. Startled, Clint and Howard spun round to see the blackness behind them split by the flashes from guns. There were yells from some of the drovers.

'Keep them pinned in the gully!' shouted Clint, afraid that with an attack at the rear the drovers might turn their attention there. 'We'll deal with the gunmen behind us.'

'There are four of them,' said Howard.

Clint grunted. 'Come on, let's get them.'

Clint crept away with Howard close behind him. They worked their way to the left of the gun-flashes and Clint was relieved to find that the repeated flashes showed no movement on the part of the four rustlers. If they moved Clint knew that the task of eliminating them would be more difficult. Time was precious, and Clint moved quickly through the darkness. The few loose stones, which were sent rolling down the hillside, went unnoticed by the rustlers intent on their task of tying down the drovers. When they were level with the four rustlers Clint paused and indicated with a wide sweep of his arm that he wanted Howard to take the man farthest up the hillside. Howard nodded and, rising to his feet, ran in a crouched position working his way upwards behind the four rustlers.

Clint turned to the nearest flash and worked his way towards it. The rustler fired again, and, noting his position, Clint rose to his feet and ran a few yards before dropping to the ground again. A short distance away loomed a boulder which, Clint realised, was being used as cover by the rustler. Clint drew a knife from the leather scabbard on the left-hand side of his belt. He crept forward and rose slowly to his feet until he could see a black form merging with the boulder. His attack must be swift and sure; the man must have no chance of warning his companions. As the rustler raised his rifle Clint sprang into the attack. His body crashed against the man taking him completely by surprise. At the same time Clint's right arm swung viciously upwards and buried the knife deep in the man's side. They fell to the ground and Clint twisted off the man's body, dragging his knife away as he did so. The rustler rolled over and lay still.

Panting for breath, the deputy sheriff pushed himself to his feet and moved slowly up the hillside, his eyes keen to catch a glimpse of the second man. The firing was beginning to die down across the hillside and correspondingly the firing from the three rustlers ahead of him had almost ceased. Clint realised that both sides knew it was useless firing at every shadow and therefore there would be attempts by both drovers and rustlers to get closer to each other. If the men above him were to slip away it would be dangerous for the drovers.

Suddenly Clint was aware of someone close at hand. Almost at the same moment the rustler sensed Clint's presence. The rustler whirled round and in that movement betrayed his exact position to Clint.

The deputy did not hesitate; he leapt at the form, his body crashed solidly against the man, but he misjudged the arc of his knife and merely nicked the man's arm. As they hit the hard ground, the man twisted quickly and brought his knee up into Clint's stomach, throwing him to one side. Clint gasped for breath and saw the man looming above him. He had kept a firm grip on his Colt and even as the rustler swung his rifle down at Clint, he fired. The bullet struck upwards through the man's stomach and the impact sent him staggering sideways whilst the momentum of his rifle took it downwards to crash hard on the rock close to Clint's head. The rustler pitched forward into a huddled silent heap.

Clint pushed himself to his feet, regretting that he had had to fire. If Howard had not dealt with the other two men they would be alerted.

As Howard crept away from Clint, he decided to go for the man highest up the hillside. He moved quickly, noting the position indicated by the rifle flash, and soon found himself behind the rustler. The man never knew what hit him as Howard brought his Colt crashing across the back of his head. Howard stepped over the unconscious form and started to creep down the hillside. He had just located the second man when there was a shout followed by the crash of a Colt further down the hillside. He saw the man turn in the direction of the voice, but was too far away to leap at him. The man raised his rifle at a shadowy form which rose from the ground a little below him. Howard squeezed his trigger and saw the rustler crash forward on to his face.

Collins stepped down the hill and saw the man was dead. He looked up at the shadowy form that was moving up the hillside.

'That you, Clint?' he called, his Colt at the ready.

'Sure, Howard,' came the reply, and a moment later the two men were face to face.

'Are you all right?' asked Howard anxiously.

'Yes,' replied Clint. 'The two that I tackled are both dead.'

'Then that leaves only one alive,' said Howard. 'The man further up is unconscious, but he'll be out cold for a long while.'

'Good,' said Clint. 'Let's get back to the drovers.'

The two men hurried across the hillside, and were soon identifying themselves to the cattlemen.

'I reckon they're trying to slip away,' said one of them as Clint dropped beside him.

'Right, take three men to the bottom of the gully, and stop anyone who tries to get that way,' ordered Clint. Four of the drovers were soon crawling down the hillside to cut off any escape of the rustlers.

Clint took the others and moved further upwards before dropping into the gully.

'Move down the hill carefully and try to drive them towards the men at the bottom of the gully. If they try to climb out of the gully they'll be silhouetted against the sky as they cross over on to the side of the hill.'

Clint and Howard, followed by the drovers, began to move slowly downwards. It was not long before the rustlers became aware of their presence and a fresh outburst of firing took place; but soon the rustlers realised the drovers had the advantage. They began to give way and moved downwards to the valley – only to be met at the bottom by the four drovers. Realising the position was hopeless, the rustlers called out their surrender, and in a matter of a few minutes the drovers had them rounded up.

'Let's git them back into camp,' said Clint. 'When we've rounded up their horses at daybreak, Howard and I will take them into Red Springs.'

Once they were in the drovers' camp, the rustlers were securely tied and Clint moved amongst them quickly.

'Mason isn't amongst them,' he said to Howard.

'He must be the one that got away,' said Howard. 'Do you think we'd better contact Dan?'

'Might take some doing,' replied Clint. 'We're not certain where he will be, but I'm sure he will be able to take care of things.'

11

When Butch Mason slipped over the edge of the hill into the gully, his mind was on the two men he had been paid to kill. From his point of view it was lucky that Seth Cunliffe had ridden into the camp. His actions had all the appearance of a man who was going to stay and this puzzled Mason, particularly as he had seen the sheriff in the camp as well. After the attacks on the other two herds, it was more than likely that the sheriff was checking on things and Cunliffe had ridden in to discuss the latest position. Mason was not a man to let this worry him. With the two drovers in camp he would finish his job all the sooner. It was more than likely that he would have to kill the sheriff as well, but Mason did not mind that. In any case it would no doubt suit Brady and that could mean more cash for him.

Mason's thoughts were shattered with a startling ferocity by the crash of a rifle to his right. Suddenly there was a fusillade of shots. There were yells behind him as the rustlers dived for cover, horses released from the straining hands of the riders, and frightened by the shots, bolted forward. Mason's cool, calculating brain raced; he mustn't be holed up in this gully. He dug his heels into his horse and sent it galloping forward in amongst the riderless animals. At the same time he slid sideways out of the saddle, holding on to it tightly, using his horse as a shield from the rifle fire. He tore down the gully, hoping his strong, powerful horse would keep its feet. A fall would send him under the trampling hooves of the horses behind him. Suddenly he realised that he was out of the gully and on to the flatness of the valley. He hauled himself back into the saddle and gradually brought his horse under his steadying hand to a slower pace. The other animals scattered around him and tore away into the darkness.

Mason turned his horse northward, and, when he was satisfied no one was following him, he brought his horse to a halt.

Firing was still going on along the hillside. Mason frowned, his thoughts troubled him. How did the drovers know they were going to be attacked? The first herd had been in this position in the valley when the rustlers had attacked at dawn. Had this one been planted in the same position to tempt the rustlers? Had someone been shrewd enough to guess their intentions to surmise that they would use the gully to reach the valley? Mason had an uneasy feeling about the whole thing. The rustlers had put the raid earlier than the previous one in order to take the drovers by surprise. The raid had been planned in camp and no doubt Howard Collins had overheard everything. Could he have escaped? Suddenly Mason's mind seized on a small point, something which had been puzzling him. Howard Collins had been captured, the sheriff was in the drovers' camp, but where was the deputy sheriff? He was known to have been at Brady's place with the other two. Could Clint Schofield have got on their trail and located the hide-out, rescued Collins and warned the drovers? How near he was to the truth Mason could not guess, but of one thing he was certain: their plans had been blown sky high. He was tempted to hang around to see the outcome of the battle, but, pinned down in the gully as the rustlers were, he was certain that the drovers would win.

Time could be precious and Mason decided that he had better warn Sam Brady. He put his horse into a steady lope northwards through Cedar Valley.

As he started to climb the rise from which he would drop into the valley in which Brady lived, Mason slowed his horse. Throughout the ride his thoughts had been preoccupied with the whole situation. Now it suddenly crossed his mind that if Howard Collins had been watching Brady's ranch, it could be possible that the ranch was still being kept under observation.

Collins had left his post in order to follow the cowboy so it would be possible that someone else had taken over the job of lookout. Against the argument, Mason realised that the cowboy had reported only three men at Brady's house, but there could have been others in the vicinity. With no definite conclusion, Mason still decided to be cautious. Instead of surmounting the rise and dropping into the valley, he turned his horse below the ridge and circled to the left, swinging round the hill until he was riding parallel to the valley. He kept checking his position by dismounting and creeping to the top of the ridge. When he found that he was immediately behind the ranch-house he left his horse, slid quickly over the skyline and made his way swiftly to the back of the house, which was in darkness. He tapped on the back door and, after about five minutes, he succeeded in making himself heard and was admitted to the house by a half-dressed, sleepy Sam Brady. He was startled to see Butch Mason, and the sight of the gunman drove all thoughts of sleep from his drowsy mind.

'What the...?' he gasped.

Mason pushed past him into the house. 'Sorry to disturb you like this, but things have gone wrong.'

'What!' Annoyance showed on Brady's face. He shut the door and glared at Mason. 'Come in here and tell me what happened.' He led the way into a large room and was about to turn the light up higher when Mason stopped him.

'I wouldn't do that,' he said, and, seeing the mixture of surprise and curiosity on Brady's face, went on quickly, 'There may be someone out there, I'm not certain, but I reckon it was better to be cautious; that's why I came the back way; my horse is over the top of the hill.'

'All right,' snapped Brady irritably, 'now cut out the melodramatics and tell me what happened.'

Mason told his story at length, missing no detail. Brady listened intently as he paced up and down puffing strongly at a cheroot. The only comments he made throughout the tale were a few grunts, but as soon as Butch had finished he swung round, threw the remains of his cheroot in the dull embers in the fireplace. His face was a mask of fury, his chest heaved as he breathed deeply, his lips were drawn tightly and his eyes narrowed with anger.

'Fools! Fools!' he hissed. 'They ruined everything, running into a trap like that. I left the rustling in their hands, but they haven't the brains to organise it correctly.'

Mason lay back in the chair watching the man who had hired his guns. He was partly amused at Brady's viciousness in blaming the rustlers, remembering how Brady himself had made no better attempt at rustling Shaun O'Grady's herd. Here was a man who thought he knew all the answers, but had to get other men to do his work, thinking that payment in money could make them infallible. Brady's ideas had run away with him and what had started as a simple idea for revenge had grown into an ambitious scheme to make him powerful and rich, but the man was too small to succeed. Mason pulled himself up; why should he criticise or think badly of Brady? He was in the glorious position of not caring whether Brady succeeded in his ambitions or not; he was to receive cash for the elimination of certain men, and, so long as he did this, he was not bothered if Brady's other plans came unstuck.

Curious, Mason put the question, 'What happens now?'

'This kills all the schemes I had,' he snapped. 'Ruined because of some no-good, careless cowboys. Do you think McCoy suspects that I am behind the rustlings?'

Mason hesitated thoughtfully. 'The fact that he called here asking about me doesn't prove a thing, but the fact that he left Collins to watch this place indicates that there was a certain curiosity about you. However, I don't think he can make any definite connection and he won't be able to prove a thing, but if one of those rustlers talks you're finished.'

Brady's face clouded. 'Then I'm definitely finished here,' he muttered. His tone suddenly changed. 'I can start again somewhere; I didn't particularly like it here. But first you and I have some unfinished business to take care of. My schemes as far as a cattle empire here may be finished, but the most important thing remains to be settled.

Mason, there are still two men for you to kill and if Sheriff McCoy gets in your way I don't mind if he becomes another notch on your gun.'

'How do you propose I get at them now?' asked Mason.

Brady picked out another cheroot from the box on the large oak sideboard. He lit it and blew a long cloud of smoke into the air. The thoughtful look on his face gradually changed to one of satisfaction. When he turned to look at Mason there was an excited gleam in his eyes which, to the hired-gun, seemed to border on the edge of insanity. He sat down in a chair close to Mason.

'I've waited for my revenge on these four men; you've done well so far, fifty per cent success. You said the sheriff was with Burt Pallister and Seth Cunliffe. Well, I propose we get all three in Red Springs.'

'What!' Mason stared in amazement at Brady. 'You'll never do it,' he protested.

'Not going soft, are you, Mason?' rapped Brady.

Mason stiffened. 'I've never gone soft and you know it. I've a job to do with a gun and I'll do it. If you've a scheme for getting these men set up for me then get on and explain it so I can work on it.'

'If one of the rustlers talks or McCoy can prove anything against me then he'll be calling here. Well, he won't find me because you and I are riding to Red Springs.'

'What about Pallister and Cunliffe?' queried Mason, somewhat mystified by Brady's vagueness.

'They'll come with the sheriff,' grinned Brady.

'You can't be certain.'

'I can,' replied Brady. 'McCoy has a pretty wife and if he knows she's in danger he'll bring Pallister and Cunliffe to Red Springs.'

Mason gasped. This man always came up with something, but Mason was not happy about this new proposal. He did not like having a woman involved in the affair, especially if her life was going to be held forfeit. Hired-gun he may be, but he did not like fighting behind a woman's skirts. He was on the point of protesting when Brady added:

'You're paid to kill Pallister and Cunliffe; leave Mrs McCoy to my care, she's only the bait.'

Mason was still suspicious of Brady's final intentions regarding the sheriff's wife but he was paid to do a job so he resigned himself to the fact that Mrs McCoy was needed to manoeuvre the men into Red Springs.

The two men discussed the idea for twenty minutes before Brady completed his dressing.

'We'll have to be careful when we leave here,' said Mason. 'If anyone is watching this place we don't want to be seen.'

'The stable has a back door,' replied Brady. 'I can take a horse out that way. I can use the buildings beyond the stable as a protection as far as a belt of trees which runs up the hillside. I reckon they'll give me enough cover to get up the slope to join you.'

'Right,' said Mason. 'Let's ride for McCoy's ranch.'

The two men left the house and whilst Mason made his way up the hillside to his horse Brady hurried to the stable. He chose his best horse and saddled it quickly. Leading it out of the back door he kept close to the group of buildings which lay beyond the stable. Arriving at the line of trees he made his way up the hillside using every available cover. When he reached the top, he found Mason waiting for him just below the brow of the hill. They paused, listening for any sound behind the ranch, but all was silent.

'If there is anyone out there we haven't been seen,' Brady whispered. He swung into the saddle. 'Let's go.'

The two men put their horses into a walk and after a mile quickened their pace in the direction of the Brazo. They rode in silence, an air of grim determination about them. When they reached the swirling waters at Wayman's Ford they urged their horses into the water. Mason's horse faltered and Mason slipped from the saddle to swim alongside, encouraging the horse to greater effort. He cursed himself for not getting a fresh horse from Brady. This one had done a lot of travelling lately. Relieved of the weight, the animal mustered its strength, battled against the tugging water, gradually fighting its way across. Mason scrambled out of the river, grabbed the reins and patted the horse's neck. He led the animal a few yards away from the river and turned to see Brady gaining the bank. They moved a short distance downstream and rested for a few minutes.

'We can't afford to wait long,' pointed out Brady, and soon the two men were back in the saddles riding north towards the Circle C.

They kept wide of the Bar X and when the mass of the Circle C buildings loomed ahead they pulled to a halt.

'What about the ranch hands?' asked

Mason. 'Mrs McCoy will need a horse and if we attempt to get one they'll hear us.'

'We take Mrs McCoy first,' replied Brady. 'If any of the outfit get nosey they won't dare try to rescue her. You get Mrs McCoy, then I'll get a horse.'

The two men proceeded cautiously to the house at a walking pace, and tied their horses to the rail. All was quiet. Brady moved quickly in the direction of the stables whilst Mason stepped quietly on to the verandah and slowly turned the knob on the front door. It was locked! He moved swiftly round the house, testing the windows, but they were all secured. Returning to the front door, he tapped on it urgently, hoping the sound would not carry to the men sleeping in the bunkhouse. There was no sound inside the house and he risked a louder knock whilst keeping his eye on the bunkhouse. A few moments later he heard the sound of an inside door being opened, and through the glass panels on either side of the front door he saw the light of an oil lamp brighten the hall. Footsteps moved towards the door and the light grew stronger. Mason drew his Colt.

'Who is it?' A feminine voice asked the question with a touch of caution.

'Mrs McCoy, I've a message for you from

your husband. It's urgent.' Mason put a note of desperate urgency into his voice and grinned when it had the desired effect.

The key in the lock turned, and the door opened to reveal an anxious, worried look on the face of the sheriff's wife.

'What is...?' Her voice trailed away when Mason pushed the door wide and she saw the glint of a Colt pointing at her. Her expression changed to one of surprised fear.

'Not a sound and you'll come to no harm,' hissed Mason. He stepped inside, shutting the door behind him. Barbara McCoy retreated. 'Get dressed quickly,' ordered Mason. 'You're riding to Red Springs.'

'What do you want?' Barbara's voice was scarcely above a whisper.

'Never mind that,' replied Mason. 'Just do as you're told and you'll be all right.'

'What's happened to my husband?' There was a note of alarm in her voice as she feared the worst.

Mason laughed. 'I don't know. I haven't seen him. Now cut out the questions and do as you're told.' He stepped forward menacingly. Barbara moved towards her bedroom. 'Leave the door open,' ordered Mason. 'Don't try to raise the alarm.'

Barbara went into the bedroom and, afraid

of what might happen, dressed quickly. When she went into the hall again the front door opened and Sam Brady walked in. Momentarily, a wave of relief swept over her, thinking that rescue had come, but her hopes were smothered when Brady spoke.

'Good work, Butch. There's no sound from the bunkhouse but we shan't have to be long; it will soon be dawn.' He turned to Barbara. 'I'm sorry to inconvenience you in this way, Mrs McCoy,' he said smoothly, 'but I'm afraid it is necessary. One thing, before we go, I want you to write a note to your husband.'

Barbara saw there would be little use in resisting these two men so she crossed the hall into a large room and took pencil and paper from a desk.

'Write the following,' instructed Brady. '"I have been taken to the saloon in Red Springs. Bring Pallister and Cunliffe there, otherwise my life is in danger."'

When Barbara had signed the note Brady told her to seal it in an envelope addressed to her husband. Once she had done so Brady told her to take up the pencil again.

'Write a note to your foreman: "I've had to leave in a hurry; take this to Dan at once."'

When this had been done and the note to

the foreman put in an envelope Brady handed them to Mason. 'Put them outside the bunkhouse so they will be seen.'

Mason hurried out of the house and when he returned to his horse Brady and Mrs McCoy were already in the saddles. They left the Circle C at a walking pace and when Brady reckoned they were out of earshot of the ranch they put their horses into a fast gallop.

Red Springs was beginning to come to life as the light of a new day flooded the town when the three riders halted their horses outside the saloon.

'Inside,' ordered Brady sharply.

Barbara swung from the saddle and crossed the boards, closely followed by Brady and Mason. The bartender, who was sweeping the floor, looked up in surprise when he saw the sheriff's wife entering the saloon.

'Mrs McCoy…!' His words stopped when he recognised Butch Mason and saw the gun in his hand. He also knew Sam Brady and was puzzled why these two men should be together bringing Mrs McCoy into the saloon at the point of a gun.

'Lock up!' ordered Brady. 'You're not open until I say so.'

'But I…' the bartender started to protest.

'Don't question what I say,' snapped Brady.

Mason stepped forward pushing the muzzle of the Colt close to the bartender's face. There was a look of fear in his eyes but he felt that, with a lady threatened, he should do something to help her. He shot a quick questioning glance at Barbara.

'Better do as he says, Charlie,' said Barbara reading the predicament in his eyes.

Somewhat relieved, Charlie stepped around Mason and hurried to the batwings where he closed and locked the doors across them.

'Good, now bring us a bottle of whisky,' said Brady. 'Over there,' he added, indicating a chair by a table in the window.

Barbara sat down and Mason took up a position so that he could see the street. Charlie brought the bottle and two glasses.

'What about the lady?' laughed Brady.

Charlie looked at Barbara who shook her head. Brady laughed even louder.

'Sorry you won't join us, Mrs McCoy.' He poured out two drinks and shoved one at Mason. 'Charlie, just behave yourself and no one will get hurt.'

Charlie moved away to the long mahogany counter which he started to rub down, nervously watching the two men. Brady eyed

Mrs McCoy.

'Wal, I reckon before long your husband will receive that note. If he does as instructed and tries no heroics you and he will be safe enough.'

Barbara made no comments. It was obvious that she was being held hostage for two men, although she did not understand the reason, but she was afraid, knowing full well that Dan was not a man to back down to threats.

12

As the sun came up filling the Texas countryside with the light of a new day three men stretched their cramped, aching limbs and concentrated their attention on Sam Brady's ranch-house. A feeling that he was near to a solution to the recent troubles seized Dan and he was eager for the appearance of Brady. Time seemed to pass slowly. Burt Pallister became restive.

'Isn't anyone going to move down there?' he said irritably. 'I'm anxious to know what's happened to my herd. I don't want to hang around here too long.'

'I know,' replied Dan. 'I'm wondering why we haven't seen anyone. We'll wait a bit longer, then if no one appears I'll go down and have a look round.'

Suddenly Seth Cunliffe grabbed Dan's arm. 'There's some hombre hitting this valley at a hard run.' He nodded in the direction of a lone horseman behind whom swirled a cloud of dust churned up by the flying hooves of his horse.

Excitement seized Dan. At last something was happening.

'Someone's in a mighty big hurry to contact Brady,' he said. He continued to watch the horseman for a few moments. 'That's Howard Collins!' he gasped.

'What's he doing heading for Brady's place?' said Pallister.

'That puzzles me,' replied Dan. He glanced back at the ranch-house. 'And what puzzles me more is why no one has appeared from the house; those hooves are beating a tattoo which would bring anyone out to see what was the matter.' He paused. Howard was closing the distance to the house rapidly. Suddenly Dan jumped to his feet. 'C'm on! I reckon we've been watching a deserted house.'

He started down the hillside followed by Burt and Seth. They reached the bottom of the slope as Howard pulled up in a swirl of dust outside the house. He swung out of the saddle to face the three men.

'Thank goodness I've found you,' he said, gasping for breath. 'Seen anything of Brady or Mason?'

'No,' replied Dan. 'We've been here most of the night and it looks as though we've been watching an empty house. What brought you here?'

Howard told them the whole story and at its conclusion there was relief in Pallister's eyes at the knowledge that his herd was safe.

'Both you and Clint have done well,' complimented Dan. 'We now know that Brady was behind the rustlings.' He looked thoughtful for a moment. 'It seems to me that the man you saw escape from the ambush was Mason. I reckon he's sneaked in here during the night, told Brady of the failure and both men have ridden out.'

'But we never heard anyone,' pointed out Seth.

'Agreed,' said Dan, 'but Mason's been smart enough to figure this place might be watched.' He turned to Pallister. 'Will you get the horses, Burt? We'll scout around to see if we can pick up a trail.'

Burt nodded. 'I'm willin' to ride along, now that the herd is safe.'

'So am I,' put in Seth.

'Thanks,' said Dan. 'I'm still mighty anxious to know if you recognise Brady.'

Burt hurried away for the horses whilst Seth and Howard started to search the ground near the house. Dan headed for the stables, figuring that Brady would need a horse to leave the ranch, and he soon found the answer to his supposition in the evidence of the fresh hoofmarks behind the stables. He followed them and, when he saw them turn up the hillside, he called to the others.

'One set of hoof-marks here,' he pointed out when the other men reached him. 'Let's see what's at the top of the hill.'

The three men hurried to the top of the hill, and a few moments later Dan shouted triumphantly when he found the second set of hoof-marks joining the first and both head in the same direction. He shouted to Burt Pallister when he appeared with the horses and soon the four men were following the trail left by Brady and Mason.

At first the trail was easy to follow, but later, when harder, stonier ground was reached, the going became slower. On more than one occasion they had to scout around for some considerable time before picking up the trail again. After about an hour and a half Dan pulled to a halt.

'This is slow going,' he said, 'and all the time, those two could be getting further away. It seems to me that they are definitely heading north and that means crossing the Brazo at Wayman's Ford. I know they could double back but I'm going to take a chance. Let's ride for the Brazo and see what we can pick up on the north bank of the river.'

The other three men agreed and they put their horses into a fast gallop. A few miles further on they had reached the top of a low hill and were turning to follow the ridge northwards when Dan pulled hard on the reins. The others halted beside him and Dan indicated a lone rider heading southwards along the low country to their right.

'That's my foreman's sit of a horse,' said Dan. 'Something must be wrong for him to be heading south at that pace.'

He drew his Colt and fired twice into the air. They saw the rider slacken pace and pull to a halt, looking in their direction. Dan waved and the four men put their horses down the slope whilst the foreman turned in their direction.

'What's brought you this side of the Brazo?' called Dan to his foreman as they pulled their horses to a halt. Dust swirled around them as the riders steadied their horses.

'I was looking for you,' replied the foreman breathlessly. 'I found this outside the bunkhouse this morning,' he added, pulling a creased envelope out of his pocket.

Dan looked mystified as he took the envelope and note. His eyes scanned the note to the foreman, then he ripped open the envelope and pulled out the letter. As the words bit into his brain his face drained of its colour. He stared almost unbelievingly at the letter.

'What's wrong, Dan?' Howard's voice cut into his thoughts.

Dan passed the note to Howard without speaking. His mind was already beginning to grapple with the problem.

Pallister, Cunliffe and his foreman looked questioningly at him.

'Brady and Mason are holding my wife hostage in the saloon, in Red Springs,' explained Dan.

'Hostage?' Cunliffe was puzzled.

Dan nodded. 'Hostage for you and Pallister.'

'What!' Both men gasped together.

'But why?' queried Pallister.

'That's what I'd like to know,' said Dan. 'What does he want with you two? This rustling must have been only a small part of Brady's schemes. After Mason reported the failure of the raid they could have got clean away but they chose to take my wife and go to Red Springs. The elimination of four trail bosses seems to have been a big thing to Brady.'

'There's only one way to settle this,' pointed out Cunliffe, 'and that's to ride to Red Springs.'

'I agree,' said Pallister. 'We can't leave Mrs McCoy in Brady's hands. But why does he want to kill us?'

'We'll find out when we get to Red Springs,' said Dan grimly.

'I'll ride for the rest of the boys,' said Dan's foreman and started to turn his horse.

'Hold it,' said Dan. 'If we arrive in force, that may endanger Barbara's life. We'll go as we are.'

The five men put their horses into a brisk trot towards Red Springs, each lost in his own thoughts.

The sun was high when the riders neared the town, and when they reached the end of

Main Street, Dan called a halt. He noted that the few people on the street made themselves scarce when they saw the arrival of the sheriff and his party. He guessed that by now it was known that the two men in the saloon were waiting for them and that a gun battle was likely to ensue.

Dan swung out of the saddle and the others followed suit. It was a grim-faced sheriff, tormented by the knowledge that his wife was in danger, who spoke to them.

'Howard, I know you think the world of your sister and I know my foreman would do anything for her, but I'm asking you both to keep out of this.'

'But I...' Both men started to protest together.

'Look at it this way,' cut in Dan. 'Brady's quarrel seems to be with Burt and Seth. Now, I'm not just going to throw them at Brady's mercy but a wrong move by any one of us would spell danger for Barbara and the more of us there are the more likely it is that Brady will get edgy and there's no telling what he might do.'

'What are you figuring on doing?' asked Howard anxiously.

'Let us face him,' urged Pallister. 'It is us he wants.'

'A lawman can't stand by and see his town turned into a battleground,' replied Dan. 'This is my affair as well as yours, and even more so when my wife is being held hostage.' He looked thoughtful, eyeing the dusty, deserted, sun-drenched street. There was a tension in the air, an atmosphere of expectancy, which could only be broken by an act of violence. It was as if the whole street was balanced on the edge of pending upheaval.

'If you want us to keep out of it,' said Howard, 'let us two go to the back of the saloon, merely as a precautionary measure; no doubt Brady will have been wise enough to see that the back door is locked, but if we are there we can cut off any retreat and we will be handy if wanted.'

'All right,' agreed Dan. 'But don't endanger Barbara by any action which isn't necessary.'

'Right,' said Howard and the two men slipped away across the end of the town to work their way by the back streets to the rear of the saloon.

'In all probability we will have to face Mason,' said Dan, eyeing Pallister and Cunliffe thoughtfully. 'I figure, if Brady's hired Mason, he'll insist on him completing his job. Brady may not interfere as he'll be watching Barbara, using her first as a means of ensuring you come here and secondly as a means of protection if things go wrong.'

'Wal, what are we goin' to do?' asked Cunliffe.

'We can't formulate any particular plan until we know exactly where Brady and Mason are and what they propose to do,' replied Dan. 'Both of you wait here.'

Dan walked into the middle of the street and began to advance with a slow measured tread. His eyes took in everything. He saw people at the windows prepared to keep out of harm's way and watch the macabre events. He felt a lonely, exposed figure as he moved slowly forward, but whatever he did he must not let the two men in the saloon see his real feelings of intense concern and fear for the safety of his wife. Outwardly he must appear calm. Suddenly the silence was broken by the shattering of glass. It came with such suddenness that it startled Dan, but almost instantaneously his brain was ice-cold when he saw the muzzle of a Colt through the broken window of the saloon. He did not alter his pace or his step.

'Hold it! Right there or your wife gets it, McCoy!' The voice was harsh and full of passion which demanded instant obedience otherwise the wildness would spill over with horrible consequences. Dan halted.

'Brady!' yelled back Dan. 'Give up this foolhardy scheme of yours; come out and give yourself up; all you'll have to face is a rustling charge. Go through with this and it could be a murder charge.'

There was a harsh laugh from the saloon. 'This isn't going to be a murder charge,' shouted Brady. 'It will be self-defence. Mason will take Pallister and Cunliffe. If you know what's good for yourself and your wife you'll keep out of it.'

Dan stiffened at this threat. He realised he was in a tough spot, torn between his duty as a lawman and his love for Barbara. Dan could not see a way out of his dilemma; he had to play for time at the moment.

'How do I know my wife is all right?' he shouted. 'Let her speak to me. Are you safe, Barbara?'

There was a moment's silence.

'Dan, I'm all right.' Dan was relieved to hear his wife's voice. 'Don't worry about me; do your duty as a lawman.'

'Don't be a fool, McCoy,' yelled Brady, obviously angry at Barbara's remark. 'One step wrong by you and your wife won't speak to you again. Send Cunliffe and Pallister up here.'

'What have you got against them? Why should I turn them over to you?' shouted Dan.

'It's justice I want, McCoy.'

'Justice? I'm the law around here,' called Dan. 'Make your charges to me.'

'You would do nothing about them,' answered Brady, 'but I'm going to make them pay for their crimes, just the same as Stevens and O'Grady have paid already. They will get a chance just the same as the other two, so that they will be killed in self-defence.'

Crimes? Dan was bewildered. These four trail bosses were tough men, hard-riding, hard-hitting, but never criminals.

'Brady, you've got me to reckon with,' called Dan grimly. 'I won't...'

'Unless Pallister and Cunliffe get up here and you get out of the way your wife will be killed,' shouted Brady.

'Even if I allow them to come to the saloon and you kill them, you'll still have me to deal with afterwards.'

Brady laughed. 'You don't give me much credit. After they've paid for their crime Mason and I get out of here taking your wife with us as an insurance for safe travel and to be sure you don't follow. We'll drop her off on the trail and you can pick her up afterwards.'

Dan knew he was caught, but his sense of duty made him stand fast. His thoughts raced; he must think of something quickly. The pound of feet cut into his brain. He turned to see Pallister and Cunliffe running towards him.

'Go back!' he yelled, but the two men took no notice.

'We had to come,' panted Pallister when they reached Dan. 'We couldn't stand by and see your wife threatened this way.'

Dan started to reason with the two men, and to the people of Red Springs it took on the appearance of a council of war.

Brady laughed when he saw the two trail bosses run down the street to join Dan.

'Looks as if things are going to work our way, Butch,' he said. 'Can you take them?'

'Sure,' replied Mason, his voice full of confidence. 'A couple of trail bosses are easy pickings. What if the sheriff doesn't hold off?'

'Wal, we've got his wife here,' remarked Brady. 'If that doesn't persuade him to keep his nose out I'll pick him off from here. Just make sure your position brings them forward towards the saloon.'

'Right,' said Mason. He drew his Colt from its holster, checked it and replaced it carefully. He flexed his fingers and then with one movement the gun reappeared in his hand. Charlie gasped at the speed of the draw. Mason slipped his Colt back to its holster and walked towards the door. Brady grabbed Barbara roughly by the arm and dragged her from her chair so that she was between himself and the window. His left arm encircled her tightly and he drew his Colt from the holster strapped to his right thigh.

'Right, Mrs McCoy, we're all ready for the showdown. Don't try anything, it will be the worse for you if you do. If your husband is fool enough to come with those two hombres you'll see him die.' He paused then called over his shoulder. 'Don't you try anything, Charlie, or Mrs McCoy will get the first bullet.'

Barbara's brain pounded. She saw only a hopeless position from which there was no way out for Dan. There was terror in her eyes as she struggled against the vice-like grip of Sam Brady. A deep chuckle sounded close to her ear.

'It's no good, Mrs McCoy, you'll have to watch.' Brady's grip grew tighter until it hurt and Barbara realised she could achieve nothing by struggling.

She looked along the street to where Dan was still in conversation with the two trail bosses.

Mason opened the saloon door and stepped outside. His slow tread echoed on the sidewalk and caused the three men to swing round to face the saloon. Mason stepped down into the dusty road and walked to the centre of the street. His presence seemed to charge the atmosphere with an extra tension. His appearance was a sign that the final act of violence was but a few minutes away. He stopped and turned to face the three men; his legs parted slightly and an almost imperceptible crouch came into his stance as he balanced himself ready for instant action. The three men watched him grimly. Dan had stood out against the trail bosses who had tried to persuade him that this was their affair, and, not wanting Barbara hurt, had wanted him to stand down. He realised they would have a better chance if Mason came to them, for at that angle Brady's gun would be less effective. His hopes of Mason coming to them were shattered when Brady split the silence with his harsh voice.

'Send Pallister and Cunliffe forward,' he

yelled, 'or Mrs McCoy gets hurt.'

The two cattlemen glanced at Dan, almost pleading with him to keep out of this affair, but he shook his head. They stood watching Mason for a few moments then, as one man, they stepped forward, each step slow and measured. Dan had placed himself on the right-hand side of the trio so that he could watch the saloon and Mason at the same time. Pallister was in the centre and Cunliffe kept to his left. They spread out across the roadway as they moved towards the lone gunman.

When he saw the three men begin to walk towards Mason, Brady's face became a mask of evil hate. 'Fool!' he hissed when he saw the sheriff had called his bluff about Barbara. 'McCoy gets it first from me and you can watch it.'

Barbara stiffened, staring wide-eyed at the advancing figures of the menacing men. Slowly, ever so slowly, the gap between them and the gunman shortened. Each man wondered if Mason would make the play first, but really knowing it was up to them. Mason's reputation for drawing in self-defence was going to be upheld even though he was outnumbered. Dan watched the window carefully, feeling that Brady would not have any qualms about shooting first. As the men came into his range Brady raised his Colt. Desperation seized Barbara. She must do something.

Suddenly she jerked her foot upwards and rammed it down sharply on Brady's instep. A gasp of pain escaped from his tight lips and his hold on Barbara relaxed momentarily. In that second Barbara acted swiftly. She jerked her arms forcibly upwards breaking Brady's grip and, before he realised what was happening, she grasped his Colt pulling it upwards with all her might. At the same time her head came down to meet his hand and she sank her teeth into it viciously causing him to lose hold of the gun. She twisted away from him, but Brady recovered quickly and swung a vicious blow which sent Barbara crashing back against the wall. The gun was sent flying across the room from her grasp. Brady leaped for the Colt, but was too late; Charlie, who as soon as he saw Barbara's effort, had started to move forward, seized the gun and swung it upwards as Brady leaped forward. With no time to aim, Charlie squeezed the trigger. A roar filled the saloon, and the bartender was aware of Brady being flung sideways as the bullet tore into his hip.

The whole incident was over in a few seconds, but the crash of the Colt was a signal for instantaneous action outside. Horror seized Dan at what that sound from the saloon might mean. Mason's gun leaped to his hand as he saw the two trail bosses dive for the ground jerking at their Colts. Two rapid shots hit the dust close to them and, before they could fire, he turned his gun on Dan who was jerked back to the immediate situation by the roar of the Colt. His hand moved with snake-like swiftness and even as Mason squeezed the trigger Dan fired. The sheriff felt a bullet tear through his shirt and felt a searing pain along his side. He fired again, but Mason's knees were already buckling under the impact of the sheriff's first shot which had bored into his stomach. Dan's second shot took Mason in the chest, sending him crashing to the ground.

Dan jumped forward, ignoring the gunman, and raced to the saloon. He burst through the door but pulled up sharply when he got inside. Howard and the Circle C foreman who, on hearing the first shot, had been seized by horror of the possible consequences and had burst through the back door, were standing over Brady who lay crippled on the floor. Dan took in the scene in a flash and jumped to Barbara's side.

'Are you all right?' he asked as he helped her to her feet.

'Oh! Dan!' she cried and burst into tears, sinking her head against his chest.

'It's all over,' he comforted. 'Charlie, bring Barbara a brandy,' he called.

A heavy silence after the sudden shattering gunfire lay on the main street of Red Springs. Pallister and Cunliffe pushed themselves to their feet and this seemed to be a signal for people to hurry from the buildings to bring more normal noise back to the street. The trail bosses hurried to the saloon where they were relieved to find that Mrs McCoy was all right.

'What happened?' they asked.

Charlie told the story quickly.

'Well,' said Dan, 'now we might get to the bottom of this whole affair.' He looked at Pallister and Cunliffe. 'Do you know this man?' he asked indicating the wounded Brady.

Pallister shook his head. Cunliffe stared hard at Brady.

'His face is familiar,' he muttered.

'It should be,' snapped Brady. 'You ruined me four years ago up in Kansas.'

Knowledge dawned on the two cattlemen. 'Then your name is really Walker,' said Cunliffe. 'A small rancher who barred our way four years ago and refused us permission to cross his land. Others backed him up. It would have meant a big detour for our herds with possible disastrous consequences. Pallister and I waited for Stevens and O'Grady to join us. Brady, or Walker, as he was then, tried to force us to back down by stringing up a drover from each outfit. We fought him, and drove our cattle straight through his land.'

'And that ruined my land,' snarled Brady.

'We'd have tracked you down, after you ran out, for what you did to our men,' said Pallister, 'but we had other problems on our hands.'

'I swore to get you four trail bosses. I got Stevens and O'Grady and I'd have got you two if it hadn't been for a meddling sheriff.' He glanced hatefully at Dan.

'I'm only sorry I didn't get on to you sooner,' retorted Dan. 'Howard, get the Doc to him and then see him into jail.' He turned to his foreman. 'Ride to meet Clint who'll be bringing in the rustlers. Tell him what's happened. I'm going to take Barbara home.'

The two men nodded. Dan turned to Pallister and Cunliffe. 'Thanks for all your help,' he said. 'Now you can bring your herds through without any fear.'